redemption

Book One in The Vaedra Saga of

The Vaedra Chronicles Series

ester lópez

chapter one

AS THE SHUTTLE flew over Plumaris, Tam could see the southern portion was inhabited by small clusters of villages among wooded or forested areas with lakes and streams flowing nearby. It was beautiful. She had heard otherwise. Finally, the shuttle moved north. The farther north they went, the more the terrain changed.

The northern portion was a desolate place. The treeless, rocky terrain was depressing. A voice came over the comms unit.

"If you look closely, you can see some definite shapes in the rocks. Buildings inside these rock formations house the single guards who patrol the area, so there's no escaping."

The shuttle set down in front of a massive door and the voice came back. "This is Leviticus Station. Welcome to the Gates of Hell."

A guard stood before her. "Let's go." He stepped between two seats and ushered her and the other two prisoners out of the shuttle.

She stood up and moved slowly out of her seat, her legs shackled and her wrists bound. The two males accompanying her were also shackled and bound, making the exit laborious.

Another guard led them toward the massive doors, while the first guard brought up the rear. Both guards were armed.

She followed behind the guard and entered through the massive doors. The place was big enough for several shuttles to fly through, but the one she arrived in sat outside the cave. The rock walls were smooth. Two more guards joined them and removed the leg shackles of each prisoner. Their wrists remained bound as they walked to a people mover. Wide enough to accommodate all of them, they stepped inside and went down a couple levels when the doors opened again. This time, the two male prisoners were escorted off with two guards. The doors closed and the three of them continued down. When the doors opened again, they got off and walked down another hall to a guard station.

"Hey, wait a minute. We were expecting a male prisoner," the guard said.

"Sorry. This is what you get," the escort guard said.

"Where are we going to put her?"

"That's up to you. We were just supposed to escort her here."

"You could release me and pretend you never saw me," Tam said.

"You wish," the guard said. "I have a place for you, but you're not going to like it."

"I don't even like being on this planet," she said.

"Let's go." The guard grabbed her arm and escorted her down another hall.

"Don't I get a unicrin or something?" she asked.

"Nope. You get nothing for free here," the guard said.

She still wore the I.S.P. unicrin from when she was arrested. In the prison on Tarsius, they at least let her cleanse herself every couple days. It would be interesting having to go through her monthly cycle without cleansing herself or having clean clothes to change into.

The guard pushed her forward farther down the hall.

"Who do I speak to about my monthly cycle?" she asked.

"Your what?"

"My monthly, you know. It's due soon." She stopped and glared at him.

"Oh, uh, I'll speak to my supervisor. He'll have to get back to you on that."

"Please do, or we'll have a hygiene problem."

He stopped at a corner and spoke to another guard. "I've got you another gem miner," he said.

"Bring him here."

"It's her," the guard said.

The other guard gave her the once over. "What are we supposed to do with a woman in here?"

"The same as the men, I suppose."

"That won't work, and you know it."

"I'll speak to Kellen about it," the first guard said. "She's your problem now."

Dram aimed the AI-powered plasma drill at the target and squeezed the handles. In a matter of minutes, liquid tulin poured into the wheeled vat below the hole. When it reached the fill line, he had the next vat lined up.

"Vat's up!" he yelled. He pushed the full vat down the track and concentrated on filling the new vat.

Gomet grabbed the vat and pushed it to the next link, where the tulin would be poured into the grand vat. From there, it would be made into coins or bars or melted into exquisite furniture.

Dram remembered when he owned furniture made of tulin and spent the coins on ships to increase his business. It had been months since he was locked up, here on Plumaris. His was a life sentence, so he was adjusting to a different way of living.

Besides, it beat the alternative.

He lined up the plasma drill once more when the flow of tulin stopped. Pressing the handles, he tried to get more tulin to pour out, but this vein was done. He reached up and pulled the sensor down to locate more of the shiny gold-colored metal.

Moving the sensor around, up and down the rock wall, it finally beeped. He marked the spot and moved his vat into place and began the same routine. More liquid tulin flowed after the plasma drill did its thing.

He couldn't imagine doing this kind of work without these tools. The only reason humans were needed was to move the vats along and to manually use the sensor. Oh, and the fact that it was penance for living a life of crime. Yeah, that's the reason.

"I heard we were getting another cellmate," Gomet said.

"Did you, now?" He pushed the filled vat to Gomet.

He walked back a distance to pick up another empty vat and push it along to his target area. He could only get so much out of a vein with one blast. He was glad he didn't have Gomet's job. It was boring as hell, standing around and waiting on someone else to do the work.

"So, when is this new cellmate coming in?" he asked. He aimed his plasma drill again and blasted another vein of tulin.

He watched the liquid pour into the vat.

"Tonight," Gomet said.

"Hmm." Gomet usually got good intel. A new cellmate didn't come along too often. It would be amusing for a while, but then he would get bored harassing the newbie. But cell-mates didn't mean they would be working together. They would just be sleeping in the same cell. Right now, it was him, Gomet, and Thadus. After this newbie, there were no more beds.

Thadus worked the gem mines. The work was harder, but

not as hot. Here, in the tulin mines, the high heat to melt the tulin into coins, bars, or furnishings kept the whole place sweltering. His tank top was grimy and worn and so were his pants. Once every six months, they were given some clean, recycled clothes and the old ones were washed and passed along to someone else. He would have to talk to someone about that. The smell was getting unbearable in their cell. Six months was too long to wait for clean clothes.

Thadus used his chisel to work the rubies out of their rock enclosure. He had an eye for detail, and this was slow, tedious work. The more he was able to pry the bigger rubies out, the bigger his bonus at the end of the month.

He hung from his harness over a wall of sparkling rubies.

Besides himself, there were two others who could dislodge the beauties in big pieces. They all wanted that bonus. He was planning on buying a pillow with his earnings. The flattened pillow he had was giving him neck pains and he dreamed of a good night's sleep.

Once a month, when the bonuses were given out, they had a small market set up where the prisoners could buy things they needed or wanted, luxury items that normal people took for granted.

"Thadus!"

He turned to see who called him. That was odd because no one ever called him. He caught a glimpse of movement below him on a ledge.

"Coming up!" a voice called out.

Within seconds, a woman was hoisted up next to him in a harness. Her hair was black with orange spikes coming out from it, reminding him of a matchstick.

"I'm Tam," she said.

"Well, I'm Thadus. I guess you're the newbie I heard talk about."

"I guess so."

"Let me show you what I'm doing and then you can attack that wall over there."

He reached above her head and pulled her rope closer to his. He showed her how to hold the chisel and the mallet, then went to work.

"It's simple, really. If you take your time and do it right, you get a bonus each month for the big rubies. If you break them, you get nothing."

"I didn't think prisoners got paid at all," she said.

"We don't. The bonus helps to buy things like a blanket or pillow or clothes. Just a little something to make our hell on Plumaris a little easier to bear."

Thadus reached up to the rope above her harness, and shoved Tam further away.

"That's the end of your lesson. You're on your own now."

"Thanks," she mumbled.

Thadus went back to work. Each ruby he extracted was carefully placed into a bag he had on his waist.

"Where's my bag?" Tam asked.

"Didn't they give you one?"

"Nope."

Thadus patted his grimy clothes and found a spare bag. He pushed off from the rock wall and slid sideways to reach Tam.

"Here. You should have gotten one when they hooked you up to the harness."

"I guess they overlooked that part," she said.

Hours later, an alarm sounded, and the harnesses were lowered to the ground.

"What's happening?" Tam asked.

"It's quitting time," Thadus said.

A guard unhooked each of them from their harness and pointed to a wall with a box protruding out from it.

"Deposit your rubies with your code over there," the guard said.

"What code?" Tam asked.

"Weren't you given a code when they processed you?"

"I don't remember a code."

"Name?"

"Tam."

"Your code is 043," the guard said. He glanced at his comm-pad. "Don't forget that number. You need it for everything."

"Yes, sir." Tam walked to the box and pressed her code into the keypad beside it and it opened. She deposited her rubies inside the box and the box closed.

"Now what?" she said.

"You go to your cell," the guard said.

"She's a newbie," Thadus said. "I don't think she has been assigned a cell yet."

"Wait there," the guard said. He pointed to a spot against the wall.

After Thadus and two others deposited their rubies and went on, the guard approached her.

"Come with me," he said.

"Is this our daily routine, then?" Tam asked.

"You came late today. Tomorrow, you eat the morning meal and put in ten hours with two breaks and a mid-day meal, then go back to your cell at the end of the day."

"Sounds like fun." Tam said, sarcastically. "But I'll need a bag for tomorrow."

"A bag?"

"You know, to put the rubies into as I collect them."

The guard gave her a side glance. Then he produced a bag for her. "Don't lose this one."

"I never had one so why would you say that?"

The guard shook his head and kept going. She followed behind, silently. They walked through the tunnel before getting into a people mover. After a few minutes, the people mover stopped, and they exited.

"This is your cell block." The guard checked his comm-pad again. "This way." He turned right and she followed him down a hall. It looked more like a building than a cave. Each cell appeared to have four men in it. There were cells on each side of the hall. The guard stopped at the last one on the right and unlocked the cell.

There was Thadus, along with two others.

"There must be some mistake," she said.

"No. This is your cell."

"Where are the women's cells?"

"You're the first, so there aren't any," the guard said.

All three men stood frozen, glancing at each other, then her, then the guard.

"You've got to be kidding," a tall Chromian said.

"Enjoy the company, boys." The guard shoved her inside and closed the cell.

"Hello, Tam," Thadus said.

Her eyes had adjusted to the light, and she could see clearer. She realized he was Caucasian and so was the other man. All three were a bit grimy and…old.

Her stomach growled, reminding her she hadn't eaten all day. She hoped there was a meal tonight.

"There's your bed," the Chromian said. He pointed to the bunk on top. It had a mattress, but that was all. No sheets, no pillow.

"Thanks," she said. She climbed up the side to get to her bunk. She was tired. But then, she remembered she had to pee. She climbed back down.

"Where's the toilet?"

All three men stepped aside, and she could see it, out in the open, with a sink beside it.

Great. No privacy. And no shower. Well, she had to go and there wasn't anything she could do about it. She just pretended they weren't there and did her business. Maybe it would get easier. But when she finished, she realized they had all turned their backs to her. Hmm. Is this what they did for each other, too?

Before she could climb up to the top bunk, the Chromian grabbed her arm.

"What are you doing here? You're just a kid."

"I'm older than I look, old man."

"Old man?" Thadus asked.

The other Caucasian laughed.

"I asked you a question," the Chromian said.

She glanced at his hand, still holding her arm, then glared into his eyes.

"I poisoned a man, sabotaged a couple ships, and tried to kill another man, is that okay with you?"

"Did you say you sabotaged a couple ships?" Thadus asked.

"That's right."

The Chromian pulled her toward him as the other two gathered around.

"I remember you. You're the one who helped us find that traitor, Berto," Thadus said.

"Yes. You were with the pirates that boarded the ship we were on," she said.

"Berto? The man with telekinetic powers?" the Chromian asked.

"That's the one," she said.

"How do you know Berto?" Thadus asked the Chromian.

"He worked for me," the Chromian said.

"Well, it looks like we all have something in common, don't we?" she said.

The Chromian turned her loose. She looked him over. For

an old man, he had a nice body, which was more than she could say for the other two.

"How do you know Berto?" the Chromian asked her.

"He killed my brother."

"Was that the incident when Berto was fourteen anos?"

"That's how old my brother was when he died," she said.

"I don't suppose you know why he killed your brother?" the Chromian asked.

All three men surrounded her now. Were they curious? Or were they planning something else?

"I'd like to know," Thadus said.

"I know his story," she said.

"But you don't believe it, do you?" the Chromian asked.

She shook her head. "I find it hard to believe, that's all."

"Tell us," Thadus said.

The Chromian turned toward Thadus. "Her brother and two others were taking turns raping Berto's sister, who was seven anos. When Berto entered the scene, he used his powers to throw two of the boys against a wall. One died instantly, the other, a few days later."

"What about the other boy?" the other old man asked.

"I heard he turned himself in after getting caught raping another child," the Chromian said.

Thadus glanced at her. "I don't think we've introduced ourselves, Tam. You know me, but this is Gomet. He was part of the pirate crew with me. And this is Dram."

"I've heard about you," she said to Dram. "You're the one who was a slave-trader."

"That I was."

"How is that different than what my brother was accused of?" Tam asked.

"I didn't rape anyone. I located people for a price. Most of my clients wanted a labor force, so that's what I brought them. What they did with them was their business. I didn't ask questions except what ages and what sex they were looking for."

"Hmm. That certainly sounds like a reputable business," she said. She crossed her arms.

"Me and Gomet got caught by the I.S.P. shortly after we boarded your ship," Thadus said.

"The I.S.P. got me shortly after that," she admitted.

Should she mention she was an I.S.P. agent for a brief period of time? She glanced at the three men and decided against it. After all, they were all in this place because of the Interplanetary Space Patrol. She only joined the agency to get close to Berto. She turned and climbed up to her bunk. She lay there, her arms folded behind her head. She had a lot of time to think since she poisoned the I.S.P. officer on Meta. Revenge meant for Berto had driven her to that decision. An innocent man was dead while Berto was free. She was living with the consequences, sitting in a prison cell on Plumaris for the rest of her life. But the rest of her life would be more tolerable if Berto had eaten the food she brought him instead of the officer.

She glanced at the ceiling and realized she stared into space. Was the ceiling transparent? The stars were beautiful at dusk and the sky was a gorgeous violet, pink and orange. She couldn't wait to see the sunrise.

A commotion down the hall drew her thoughts away from the sky. She sat up in bed and glanced around. She could barely make out a cart being pushed by a couple prisoners, followed by two guards. She smelled food. "Is this our evening meal?" she asked.

"You better have your plate ready," Thadus said.

"What plate?"

Her three cellmates had lined up along the bars, holding metal plates. One at a time, they held out their plates through a thin slit in the middle of the door. She quickly climbed down from her bunk.

"Where do we get our plates?" she asked her cellmates.

"Well, well. What have we here?" one of the prisoners asked.

"Well, hey darlin,' no plate, no food," the other prisoner said.

She glanced at the guards. "I just arrived today. I wasn't given a plate, but I am hungry."

The guard nudged one of the prisoners. "Give it to her," he said.

The prisoner reached under the cart and pulled out a metal plate and an eating implement and handed it to her, after filling the plate with food.

"Thanks," she said.

"That's all you get," the prisoner said.

The other prisoner handed her a beverage in a metal cup. "If you want water, use the sink."

"Is the water drinkable?" she asked.

"It won't kill you, if that's what you mean," he said.

She turned and sat on the floor to eat her meal. The floor was quite dirty. *Did they ever clean it?* Her cellmates all sat on the bottom bunks of the two beds. She ate her food gratefully. It was trew, but it was made with real ingredients, not the food paste she had on the I.S.P. ship. When she finished, she rinsed off her plate in the sink. "Where do we keep these?" she asked no one in particular.

Dram pointed to a pouch on the side of her mattress.

"Thanks." She climbed up on her bunk and stowed her items in the pouch. Then she lay back down and stared at the stars.

This was the first time she didn't have a goal or plan. So far, this prison life wasn't so bad. If all she had to do was chisel out rocks all day, she could handle that.

She tossed and turned trying not to think of her brother as she slept. How could her brother be so cruel to a little girl he didn't know and then be kind to her? Maybe there were signs, she just hadn't seen them.

Her father was a different story altogether. He had been cruel to her as far back as she could remember. It started before her mother died with the nightly visits and the touching when she had been four anos. Then he started gambling and coming home drunk. She tried hiding from him, but he always found her.

She curled up into a ball, trying to forget, but the thoughts kept coming. The faces of the men her father brought home from time to time when he lost. She had been the prize. Nights were always hard for her. Then she realized, her brother had become just like her father.

Dram lay in his bunk. He was beat as usual, but for some reason, he couldn't sleep. No, that wasn't true. It was Tam that kept him up. This young girl needed a cell of her own. She didn't belong here, but she committed crimes like the rest of them. She was a distraction, that's all. He would speak to the guards about this. Something had to be done. They needed to move her to a different cell or even on the other side of the mountain. There were mines there as well, weren't there? He turned over onto his side facing the wall where Tam slept. He heard the squeaking mattress springs and watched her toss and turn, finally curling into a ball, facing him. He thought he heard her sobbing. Should he wake her? That would just embarrass her. He would observe her for now. This girl must have had a hard life. He faced the ceiling from his bottom bunk, glancing at the stars until he fell asleep.

chapter two

THE NEXT MORNING, Tam climbed down from her bunk first to use the toilet. The increasing daylight through the transparent ceiling woke her. She splashed water on her face. When she realized the others were still asleep, she climbed back up to her bunk. Maybe she would finally get some sleep. She dozed off until a loud, blaring alarm went off. She sat up in bed and glanced around. Dram and Gomet stirred. She turned toward her wall to give them privacy and catch a few more minutes of sleep.

Another few minutes brought the clanging of the plates against the bars. She grabbed her plate and implement and climbed down from her bunk. She joined her cellmates at the bars. She caught a glimpse of Dram whispering something to the guard. Then the guard glanced right at her. She swallowed hard. What did Dram just tell him? But the guard said nothing to her. She took her food and sat on the floor to eat. What she would give to have some capu right now. She drank her juice and was thankful she had food. Something scurried across the floor and it made her jump. "What was that?" she asked.

"A drizit. They're looking for food. Make sure you rinse

your plate and implement well, or you'll find them in your bed," Dram said.

She realized she would be giving up a lot by being in this place. Her life was no longer her own. After her sleepless night, though, she was thankful for Berto. Yes, if it wasn't for Berto, she would still be living in hell with her father.

"You must have had one hell of a dream last night," Thadus said to her. Her heart skipped a beat.

"Why do you say that?" she asked, trying not to look surprised.

"The squeaky springs under your mattress gave it away," Thadus said.

"It was more like a nightmare," she said. She stood to wash her plate and implement. "Are you all lifers?" she asked.

The three of them stood to rinse off their plates. "Yes, we are," Dram answered.

"From what I hear," Thadus began, "we'll be in this prison until we die."

"Well, that puts a damper on my plans," she said.

"You got plans?" Gomet asked.

She rolled her eyes.

"That was a joke, Gomet," Dram said.

"That wasn't funny," Gomet said.

"What isn't funny?" Thadus asked.

"This life. We've all done some terrible things to get here. It's supposed to be a time to think on those things and be sorrowful."

"Well, I'm finished thinking on those things," she said. "It's time to move on."

"Move on to where?" Thadus asked.

"The next step," she said.

"There is no next step," Dram said. "There's working, eating, and sleeping. That's it."

"Well, everyone in the universe is doing the same thing

right now, whether they are here on Plumaris, or somewhere else. I'll find something else to do." She had to. She couldn't face another night like last night.

After everyone took care of their bodily needs, a guard came to escort them to their workstations.

"Hey, is there anything to read around here?" she asked the guard. She read Jardan on his name tag.

"Read? Like what?"

"Stories, articles, anything written by another human," she said.

"Hmm, no one ever asked me that. I'll check around and see if I can find something for you," Jardan said.

"Thanks." She was back working with Thadus in the ruby mines. The work wasn't too difficult, but she couldn't imagine doing this exact same thing for fifty years or more with nothing else to look forward to. One thing she learned from her short time being an I.S.P. agent was that reading kept her mind busy. She needed something to take her mind off her past. She didn't want to go back to those dark places she had been mentally, when she was a child.

While she dug out her rubies, she remembered what Thadus had told her about the bonuses at the end of the month. She definitely wanted a pillow and a blanket.

"Kellen, we need to do something about the woman on Level A," Jardan said.

"We aren't set up for women here. I've put in a request to move her to another facility," Kellen said.

"Have you heard back?"

"Not yet."

"She's also asking for reading material."

"What?"

"Yes, anything written by another human."

"Geez. Next, she'll want to cleanse herself every day."

"Well, the men have been asking for that for a while now," Jardan said.

"Do they think they are staying at a luxury hotel?" Kellen asked.

"How long do you go without cleansing yourself?" Jardan asked.

"I cleanse myself daily."

"Well, what's so bad about the prisoners doing that daily? I mean, they aren't going anywhere, right? What would it hurt? Besides, the smell is strong in those cells after a couple days," Jardan said.

"They are being punished for their crimes. They lost all their rights and privileges."

"I'm talking simple hygiene. They are putting in ten-hour days as it is. They get no unicrin, bedding or pillows when they get here. I know we can afford it," Jardan said.

"Jardan, there's nothing I can do about it now. It's up to the warden and his superiors."

"Yes, sir."

Tam was back in her harness, cutting out a large ruby when the cramping started. It was always mild, but what followed was not pleasant and her unicrin was white. Strapped in tight, she continued to work, knowing she had to deal with the clean-up somehow.

By the end of the day, the harness was lowered, and the guard helped her out.

"You're going to need to sanitize this harness before anyone else uses it," she said.

"Oh, on whose authority?"

She pointed to the stain in the bottom.

"Did you wet your pants?" the guard asked.

"No."

He gave her the once over, but she walked away. The darkness of the mines hid the reality. She was able to slip out without drawing any more attention to herself. As she walked with Thadus and the guard back to their cell, someone called out her name.

"Tam!"

She turned toward the familiar voice behind a set of bars.

"What are you doing here? Did you take out the man who killed your brother?" her father asked.

"No, but I did find out my brother was a pedophile, just like you!"

The men in the cell turned toward her father.

"Did he tell you he raped me when I was four anos? Did he tell you he killed my mother when she tried to stop him?" Her hands closed into fists. "My brother was a monster, just like you!" she shouted.

Thadus ushered her to their cell. Moments later, she heard the sound of men fighting. The guard quickly locked them in and ran toward the other cell.

"Good gosh, Tam, what happened to you?" Thadus said.

She turned around. "That bad, huh?"

"Your clothes look like someone died in them."

"It's my monthly. I warned the guards, but they didn't think it was important."

An alarm went off. Shortly after that, Dram and Gomet arrived. She felt drenched in blood. It looked far worse than it felt, but what could she do?

Dram glanced at her and immediately shouted, "Guards!" He waved his arm through the bars. "Guards!"

Two guards came running up to the cell.

"What is it?" one of the guards asked.

"We have an emergency here," Dram said. He pointed at her.

"Good Lord! What happened?"

She rolled her eyes. "I warned the two guards who brought me here."

The two guards escorted her back down the hall. The front and back of her unicrin was now covered in blood.

"Can I just get some hygiene products and cleanse myself. Please?"

They brought her to an office.

"Stand here. Don't sit," one guard ordered. The other guard left and came back with two other guards. One she recognized as Jardan.

"Damn!" Kellen said. "Take the shuttle to my house and bring my mate. Tell her what's happened."

"Yes, sir." Jardan left.

Tam crossed her arms. She read Kellen's name tag. This will take a while, she thought. "Will I get to eat? I'm pretty hungry," she said.

"Yes, yes, you'll get to eat. One of the guards told me you spoke to a prisoner earlier. What was said between you?"

"What does it matter?"

"The prisoner is dead, so I need to know what happened."

"I called him out as a pedophile."

"And how do you know this?"

"Because he was my father and he deserved to die."

"I see," Kellen said. "You know you put us in a predicament."

"Really? How's that?"

"We aren't set up for women prisoners."

"I see that. What I don't understand is why you couldn't put a cleansing unit in each cell. I mean, all this kashish you're making off slave labor should afford some type of hygiene in this place. And why can't you supply each prisoner with a pillow and some bedding? Aren't we working hard enough for you? Shouldn't we at least get a good night's sleep, since we'll be spending the rest of our lives here?"

"You're asking a lot for a prisoner," Kellen said.

"Not really. I'm just asking for what any human would want after a hard day's work."

"You forget you are being punished."

"I get it. The rest of my life, I will work hard to compensate the family I've wronged. Is it too much to ask for clean clothes and a cleansing unit? Have you smelled those men lately?"

After a few more minutes, Jardan returned with Kellen's mate.

"Oh, Kellen, what's happened?" a woman said as she walked into the room.

"I've done nothing, Marla. Can you please help this prisoner?"

"Sure. Come with me, honey." Marla took Tam to the far end of the hall. There were rows of cleansing units lined up against a wall.

"Go ahead and cleanse yourself. When you finish, put these on," Marla said. She handed Tam some clothes and some hygiene products.

"Thank you," Tam said.

While she washed and dried herself off in the unit, she wondered about this woman. She seemed genuine. Was it any better at a woman's prison? When she felt human again, she stepped out of the unit and Marla walked her back to Kellen's office.

"Thank you," Tam said to Kellen.

"For what?"

"For giving me back a little dignity."

Marla smiled, while Kellen grimaced.

"There's your food." He pointed at a tray on his desk. "When you finish eating, Jardan will escort you back to your cell."

Tam sat in a chair beside his desk, putting the tray in her lap. She ate quickly. Not because she wanted to get back to her cell, but because the vibe she was getting from the two

mates was palpable. She wanted to get the hell out of the office.

When she returned to her cell, her cellmates were lying on their bunks, staring at the ceiling. Dram sat up.

"Oh, here are some reading materials," Jardan said. He pulled some rolled-up magazines out of his jacket pocket and handed them to her.

"Thanks," she said.

"What's that?" Dram asked.

"PRMs," Jardan said.

Dram looked puzzled.

"Portable Reading Materials. Inmates aren't allowed to have comm-pads. These were hard to find." He locked the door and left.

"You want one?" she asked Dram.

"Sure, why not."

She handed one to Dram.

"How'd you get new clothes and wet hair?" Gomet asked.

"Kellen's mate brought these for me and let me cleanse myself before putting them on." Her new clothes were a worn t-shirt and some stretchy, long pants.

"How decent of them," Thadus said.

"What's in the container?" Gomet asked.

She had been clutching the container since she left Kellen's office. "Hygiene products, if you must know." She climbed up to her bunk above Thadus' bunk.

"Can I have one of those PRMs?" Thadus asked.

She leaned over her bunk and handed one to Thadus.

"Thanks," he said.

"Just for the record," she began. She flipped through one of the colorful PRMs. "I put in a word for everyone's benefit."

"Oh?" Dram said.

"Yes. I told Kellen the smell around here was quite pungent."

A pillow hit her in the face. She sat up. Dram stood staring at her, his hands on his hips. "We smell?"

"Yes, and thanks for the pillow."

He reached for it, but she pulled it out of his reach. Dram jumped up and tried to grab it, but she stuffed it under her back. In seconds, she felt the bed shake. When she looked up, Dram had climbed up to her bunk. He was on top of her, his face close to hers. "I'll take that," he said. He wrapped his arms around her and lifted her off the pillow with one arm and pulled the pillow out with the other.

"Do you know how long I worked for this pillow?" he whispered.

"Tell me." She whispered back. Their faces were close and a spark of electrical energy shot through her. *Did he feel it, too?*

"Too long," he said. He tossed the pillow onto his bunk from across the cell, then backed off her and the bed.

The few moments of his nearness brought warmth to her body. She realized how cold she was when he backed away. These newer clothes were comfortable but not as warm as her I.S.P. unicrin had been. Maybe it had been the cleansing unit's water that cooled her off. Anyway, she hadn't been that close to a man in years. At least, not willingly. The more she thought about it, the more she realized she never had a meaningful relationship with any man before. At least not one she wanted to remember.

Dram watched her from his lower bunk. The thought of kissing Tam had crossed his mind. All he wanted was his pillow, but after holding her, he realized she was the first woman he held in his arms since Emma and that was so long ago. When Emma wouldn't join him, he never let another woman enter his mind or his heart.

The next morning's routine was the same as before. Tam got up earlier to take care of her needs, then crawled back into bed until the alarm sounded. Breakfast came and went, and she was back on the job.

The first thing she noticed was her harness was different. "Did you clean this harness from yesterday?" she asked the guard.

"It's new. We had to burn the last one. Next time, warn us in advance."

That's hard to do. "I'll try." She worked hard on digging out rubies. She wanted a pillow. The thought of what transpired the night before made her smile. By mid-day, she was ready to eat. The rest of the day was like the day before, but when it was quitting time, that's when things changed.

She was back in her cell with the others. She lay on her bunk as Dram and Thadus paced the floor of the cell. Her stomach growled and she heard someone else's stomach make the same noise.

"Something's happening," Dram said. He pressed his face against the bars. "All I can see is people moving out of their cells."

"Is that normal?" she asked.

"Only once a month when we get to cleanse ourselves," Dram said.

"Yes, but it's only been a couple weeks," Gomet said.

"You cleanse yourselves once a month?" she asked.

"I smell food," Thadus said.

Several long minutes later, the guards moved to the cell next door.

"They're being taken to the cleansing compartments," Dram said.

"Is that a fact?" Tam asked. She picked up her PRM and thumbed through it. The smell of food made her stomach growl again. A few minutes later, the cell next door was served their food.

Dram, Gomet, and Thadus had their faces pressed against the bars. "They're back," Dram announced.

"Our turn," Thadus said.

The guards unlocked their cell and escorted all of them to the cleansing units. Tam grabbed her container with hygiene products and fell in line with the others. When they got to the units, they were given a set of clean clothes, all of them matching in color. After cleansing, they were handed a set of sheets, a blanket, and a pillow.

"What's the occasion?" Dram asked.

"We are tired of getting complaints. Once a week, you will turn in the dirty sheets and get a new set," the guard said.

"What about the clothes? Thadus asked.

"You'll get a fresh set daily when you head to the cleansing compartments."

"Daily cleansing?" Dram asked.

"Yes. The cells apparently stink," the other guard said.

"Here," the first guard handed something to Dram. "Use this to sterilize your mattresses and old pillows before putting the new sheets on.

Dram turned and glanced at Tam. She shrugged her shoulders.

Once they sanitized everything, their food arrived. The four of them ate then made their beds.

"I'm going to sleep good tonight, Gomet said.

"Me, too," Thadus said.

She didn't want to mention that the temporary prison cells at the I.S.P. station came with bedding, pillows, and a unicrin.

But she would at least be comfortable when she slept. The

problem was trying to sleep without the recurring nightmares from her past. She rolled over to face the wall, once the lights were out. Then she heard a whisper in her ear and felt the warmth of someone's breath.

"Sleep tight, little one."

She opened her eyes and turned to see Dram's head above the side of her bunk. He touched her nose with his finger and turned to leave, but she was quick to grab his wrist. He didn't pull away.

"Thanks," she said. Mariposas jumped in her belly, when they exchanged glances. She released her grip, and he walked back to his bunk. Why would he do that? Was he thankful for being able to cleanse himself? Or did he appreciate the new bedding? She watched him a few minutes before turning away.

Something was happening between them, but she didn't know what it was. Maybe it was her imagination. Without having something to compare it with, she had no idea. She pulled her new sheet and blanket over her shoulder as she turned to face the wall. She pictured his face once more as he tried to retrieve his pillow earlier and fell asleep, thinking of Dram.

Dram lay in his bed, thinking about what this woman was doing here in Leviticus Station. He already felt punished for slave-trafficking. He had made a good living off it all those years. The people he sold were just products. He never gave them a second thought. So why was he thinking about it now? Was it something Tam had said when she first arrived? Or was it something she had done? He remembered she tried to kill Berto for killing her brother. Her brother had raped Berto's little sister. Berto himself had told him that story years ago. But for someone to hold a grudge like revenge for so long and then not act resentful, there must be more to the story. Was it that she didn't know how evil her brother was? The one thing he had never done was to take advantage of any of the young women or girls that he captured. They were off limits to him and his men. The house maidens were another thing. He let his men take them whenever they wanted. He had to keep them happy so they wouldn't touch the products he was selling. He glanced up at Tam's bunk. He wanted to learn more about this new cellmate.

chapter three

DRAM THOUGHT about what Thadus had heard her say to the prisoner down the hall. How could anyone do that to a child? Let alone, their own daughter? Well, his cellmates took care of him. And what was he thinking? It was not like him to show emotion to anyone. He didn't even show emotion to his son, Adam.

Why did he touch her nose and speak softly to her? What was it about her that made him do stupid things? He thought back on his brief time with Emma, Adam's Earthen mother. Had he been that stupid? She was the first and only woman he ever loved. Maybe he was stupid. He mated with her and knew she would bear him a son, but she refused to go with him when he finally got a salvage ship to rescue him.

Tam was the first woman he had shown any kind of affection to, in all that time, and it wasn't much. Prison was no place for a woman or relationships. She had to go. He would speak to Jardan about it in the morning.

Marla stood before the prison reform committee. "I think you will see a difference in production in a short time," she said.

"How do you know that?" Admiral Whitson asked.

"When you've had a good night's sleep, don't you feel as though you could take on the world the next day?"

"What makes you think they would feel that way?" Ms. Montooth asked.

"It's simple human behavior. We've been studying the effects of deprivation and fulfillment in our research labs on Vestra Major. And after meeting with the Earthen Delegation from the prisons on Earth, we've learned more things."

"And what's this next phase you have here?" Denton asked.

"To install a cleansing unit in each cell. That will save time in the long run. They can cleanse themselves in their own cells before or after meals. There would be privacy for each cellmate," Marla said.

"They are being punished for crimes. Why would we worry about their privacy?" Montooth asked.

"It's not so much the privacy, but the fact they can utilize their time more wisely in their own cells. It would create less work for the guards."

"How are we supposed to get this accomplished?" Admiral Whitson asked.

"We have all the manpower we need. We just need the supervision of an engineer," Marla said.

"That can be arranged," Denton said.

"What about the program that's in place now?" Montooth asked.

"Which one?" Marla asked.

"The one where they can buy a pillow or blanket with the bonuses they earn?"

"That can be upgraded to where they can earn a bonus of credits to trade in for things like sweets, books, food or beverages they don't usually get in their meals," Marla explained.

"I think we should think about all these changes before deciding anything," Montooth said.

Marla had a feeling that Montooth would be a problem for all of them. Just getting Kellen to agree on sheets and pillows was the hardest thing she had to deal with up to this point. And it wasn't Kellen so much as the warden. He put a stop to anything good the committee had tried to do in the past. He was definitely not a humanitarian.

"We've been dragging our feet long enough," said Admiral Whitson. "All in favor?"

Marla, Denton, and Whitson raised their hands.

"Well, Montooth? What have you got to say?" Whitson asked.

"I don't like it. They are being punished for committing crimes. I don't think we should make it easy for them."

"This won't make their work any easier, just their life after work," Marla said. Now, they must convince the warden.

The day started out as usual for Tam. Now that she had a pillow, sheets and blanket, what else did she need? More reading material? More hygiene products? Maybe there was a list somewhere. She would save up for something. She worked hard, getting at the larger rubies and wedging them out of the rocks.

When it came time for the mid-day meal, they all ate outside on the shaded patio. She enjoyed the pleasant Plumaris atmosphere. All the surrounding mountains had a purple hue to them that faded into pinks and reds, depending on how the sun's rays hit the mountains. When it was time to get back to work, she felt invigorated.

"Thank you for the sunshine," she said to Jardan.

"Uh, you're welcome?"

"Tell me, is that a glass ceiling in our cells?" she asked.

"No. Those are holograms, set to show you the night sky

by the corresponding hour, up until daylight to help you get sleep," Jardan said.

"Nice touch, then," Tam said. She followed the other guard back to her work site.

After she got back into her harness, the guard over the ruby mines hoisted her up and she began her tedious chisel work. A slice of rock broke off and she caught it before it fell. It had a white underside, different from other pieces of rock. She stroked it against the hard surface of the mine and it left a white mark. "Hmm." She pocketed the shard. Maybe she could use it to keep track of her days here, or at least she could keep track of her monthly. The more she chiseled, the more the rock changed. Finally, a big hunk fell below her.

"Watch out!" she yelled.

"Hey!" the guard shouted back.

"The rock is different here," she called out.

"Keep working," the guard yelled up at her.

"Whatever you say, boss," she mumbled. She tapped the rock surface a little harder and more pieces fell away. There were no rubies visible in the area, but she felt compelled to chip away at the softer rock surface. It finally exposed part of a large geode with red crystals in a circular pattern. The geode was so large, she could almost crawl into it.

"Thadus! Give me a hand, will you?" she called out.

"Oh, my worlds! What a find. Don't break them off," he said.

"How do I get this out?"

"We'll tap around the geode. That should bring quite a bonus."

The two of them worked on the bottom and moved to the top, chiseling around it. It took most of the afternoon. By late afternoon, they were able to break it free, with all the crystals intact.

"Bronin!" Thadus called out to the guard.

"What the Vaedran hell is that?" the guard asked.

"This is our bonus for the month," Thadus said.

"Yeah, we're sharing this one," Tam added.

Bronin lowered the two harnesses while they hung on to the giant egg-shaped geode. "Move to the scanner," Bronin ordered.

Tam stood with Thadus in front of the scanner, while still in their harnesses. After they were scanned, they set the geode down on the table while Bronin called for his supervisors.

Once the supervisor acknowledged their find, they were hoisted up to continue their work.

"That was exciting. Did you ever find a geode before?" Tam asked Thadus.

"No. That was a first for me. It was a beauty, wasn't it?"

"Yes. Do you think there are more, here?"

"I guess we'll find out," Thadus said. He went back to work on his area, while she continued with her area.

There were no rubies in sight, so she continued working on the softer rock. She was able to locate a smaller geode, but this one had pink crystals. Carefully, she worked it out of its encasement. She reached behind it and felt another smooth, roundish object. Could it be another geode?

Tam quickly placed the geode into her pouch. When she glanced at the cache behind where the geode had been, it looked more like a nest of eggs than rocks or geodes. None of which had been smooth like this egg-looking thing. It appeared several had hatched, but this single egg. All sat in a nest made of straw and sticks. That was the largest bird egg she had ever seen.

She lightly tapped it and heard it tap back. She glanced around the nest area and realized it had been hollow. She pulled herself as close as she could to get a better look. Light streamed into the area from the far left.

"Thadus, I see daylight," she called out.

"What are you talking about?"

"Come here!"

Thadus pushed off from his wall and moved toward her.

"Is that what I think it is?" Thadus asked.

"Um, it looks like a large egg to me," Tam said.

"Yes, but eggs that large can only be one thing," he said.

"Well, this one wants out," she said.

"What do you mean?"

She tapped the egg lightly and it tapped back. This time, the shell cracked and opened.

"Thadus, what is that?"

He glanced at her. "A dragon, Tam."

Thadus caught it in his hand when it broke free and handed it to her. "He's your find."

She glanced at it. "What do I do with it?"

"Let's see what the guard says."

"Wait! Let's keep this to ourselves. He doesn't have to know, does he?"

"They grow pretty big."

"He's kind of cute," Tam said. She petted his head.

"Yeah? Well, they eat meat, and he's probably hungry."

"Hey, this one has wings," she said.

Bronin shouted, "What are you two doing?"

"We thought we had another geode, but it turned out to be nothing but rock," Thadus said. He pushed away and returned to his work.

Tam slipped the tiny dragon into her pouch. She counted the broken eggshells. There were eight total. Seven baby dragons escaped through that hole. If the mother came in to lay the eggs, it must be big enough to climb out of.

Tam carefully continued her work, trying not to hurt the tiny dragon.

Finally, Bronin lowered them to the ground. She put her crystals on the table for Bronin to measure and weigh.

Tam kept quiet about the dragon, reaching her hand into the pouch to pet it.

"It's break time." Bronin led them out onto the patio, where there were some snacks and drinks. All the other inmates were also on break.

Tam pretended to eat her snack but put some into her pouch for the dragon. She thought she heard it squeal, but the noise of everyone talking drowned out the sound.

'It's okay, baby dragon. It's going to be okay,' she said with her mind.

"How big do these things get?" she whispered to Thadus.

"As big as a mountain," he said.

Dram and Gomet joined them. "What are you whispering about?" Dram asked.

She motioned him to come closer, so he did. She opened her pouch and showed him her find.

"Where did you find that thing?" Dram asked.

"It was in a nest with other broken eggs. This one wanted out right away," Tam said.

While she ate and fed the dragon, she thought of a name. She checked to see if it was a female. "I'll call her Ruby, since I found her in the ruby mines."

"Good choice," Thadus said.

When the break was over, they were returned to a different area.

"Hey, what gives?" Thadus asked.

"We're moving you to another area for mining," Bronin said. Another guard led the four miners to a different area. This one didn't have the rubies they had hunted, but pink crystals were stuck in the rocks.

"Are these valuable?" Tam asked.

"Yes, they are, but not as valuable as the rubies," Bronin said.

Once everyone was back in their harnesses, they were

hoisted up to the rock wall where they began chiseling for the crystals.

Tam slipped her hand into the pouch to pet Ruby, every now and then. She spoke to Ruby telepathically to make sure she was okay. She didn't want to let anyone know she had this tiny creature, for fear of never seeing her again, or worse.

~

Kellen met with his supervisory guards about the new find.

"Well, our only female prisoner managed to find the mother-load of rubies in a giant geode." He pulled the cover off the geode to let them get a good look at the prize. "She's sharing the credits with Thadus."

"Wow, that ought to give them a bonus for life," Jardan said.

"Not so fast, Jardan. I think I'll let them have bonuses for a couple months, but that's it. They can have up to ten credits each for two months each."

"And what's the second thing you wanted to tell us?" another supervisory guard asked.

Kellen re-covered the geode. "The warden is coming to inspect this place in the next day or so. I expect everyone on their best behavior. Have the inmates clean their cells and toilets tonight."

"Are we doing cleansings again tonight, sir?" Jardan asked.

"No. The inmates are clean enough for inspection," Kellen said.

"What about haircuts? The inmates are overdue for those," Jardan said.

"They can wait until after the inspection. The inmates are already getting more than they have ever had in the past," Kellen said. "You're dismissed."

~

Finally, the day was over and all the miners turned in their rubies and crystals. Bronin led them out to their cell blocks. Tam kept Ruby in her pouch and petted her. Ruby seemed content to curl up in her bag.

Once she was inside her cell, Bronin announced that there wouldn't be cleansings tonight.

"Why not? I thought this was going to happen every night?" Thadus asked.

"There's been a change in plans," Bronin said.

"What change?" Dram asked as he entered the cell with Gomet.

"Tomorrow, you will all be cleaning your cells and toilets. The warden is coming to inspect this place."

"What about our haircuts?" Gomet asked.

"We haven't had one in six months," Dram said.

"Yeah. Orders from the top. You'll get your haircut after the inspections."

"What did you do this time?" Dram asked Tam.

"Why do you think I had anything to do with it?"

"None of this happened before you came along," Dram said.

"Yeah," Gomet agreed.

"Are you complaining?" Tam asked.

"Not at all," Dram said.

Then he noticed her hand. "What's that?"

"Oh, this?" she asked. "This is Ruby, my dragon, remember?"

She showed Ruby to Dram and Gomet.

"The hell you say," Gomet said. "You're thinking of keeping it?"

"She found a nest of dragon eggs while working the ruby mines. They all had hatched but this one. Plus, she found the mother-load of rubies in a geode as big as she is," Thadus said.

"You've been busy today," Dram said.

"That I have," she said.

"How long are you keeping Ruby?" Gomet asked.

"I don't know. She bonded with me, so until she gets too big to hide, I guess."

"You know they get really big, right?" Dram asked.

"I was told that, yes."

"And they eat meat," Dram added.

"I was told that, too."

"Well, *you* are meat to them," Dram added.

"I hope to train her to eat other meat," Tam said.

"Good luck with that," Dram added.

Tam petted Ruby and whispered to her until it was time to eat. When the guards and prisoners brought their food, she shared what she had been given with Ruby by letting her eat from her dish.

Afterward, she showed Ruby where the toilet was and explained to her how to use it.

"You actually think that thing is listening to you?" Dram asked her.

"That thing's name is Ruby. And yes, I think she can understand me. She seems very smart," Tam said. Tam sat Ruby on the edge of the toilet seat. Ruby clung to the edge of the seat with her back legs and leaned forward. She drizzled into the toilet. *'I am very smart,'* a female voice came into Tam's head.

"See that. She is smart," Tam said to Dram. She scooped up Ruby and headed to her bunk. She set Ruby on top of the bed, then climbed up herself. She put Ruby on her belly and spoke to her telepathically. *'Did you speak to me a little bit ago?'* Tam said with her mind.

'Yes, I did. If I spoke to you with my voice, you wouldn't understand me. My vocal cords haven't developed yet.'

Tam ran a finger down the spines on Ruby's head and back. *'I love your beautiful scales, Ruby. They look iridescent in the light. Even the ridges on your head seem colorful. And your green eyes look almost human.'*

'Thank you. I'm growing fond of you, too.' Ruby responded.

'You are doing quite well for a newborn,' Tam said.

'Thank you. Can you tell me how many siblings I have?'

'There were seven other eggs besides yours. You hatched after the others, so I don't know how many brothers and sisters you have.'

'If it's possible, can I see the others at some time?'

'I don't know where the rest of them went or when they hatched. I haven't told anyone about you except my cellmates.'

Ruby jumped off Tam's belly and curled up near her pillow and went to sleep.

Tam thought about the tiny creature. Ruby's underbelly was yellowish-white, while the rest of her was dark gray with the iridescent highlights. Her front legs were shorter than her back legs, but she used them for crawling and holding her food while she ate. Her nostrils were large and her beak was wide. Just how big was Ruby going to get? Tam rolled over and went to sleep.

By morning, Tam woke earlier than her cellmates and took care of her needs. When she climbed back into bed, she watched as the tiny creature flew from the bed and down to the toilet. Apparently, Ruby took care of her needs as well, then flew back up to the bunk with Tam.

'Very good! You amaze me, Ruby. You learn so fast. I'm proud of you.'

'Thank you. Aren't we getting up for the day?'

'We'll sleep a little longer until the alarm goes off, then we'll get up.'

Ruby curled up near Tam's head and they both drifted off

for a few minutes more. When the alarm, finally went off, Tam reassured Ruby that they had a few more minutes before the food arrived.

Once the guards and prisoners came down the hall with their food, Tam had Ruby in her pouch.

After getting their morning rations, the guards announced a change in their daily routine.

chapter four

"WHAT DO YOU MEAN, there's a change in plans?" Dram asked.

"You forgot already?" Jardan said. "You will be cleaning your cell and your toilet. We'll bring you a broom and scrub brush."

Thadus glanced at Dram. "It's your turn to clean the toilet. I did that last time, remember?"

"Yeah, yeah, don't rub it in," Dram said.

Jardan left the area. Shortly afterward, another guard brought them a broom, a dustpan, and a brush for the toilet. "Don't we get some chemicals to clean the toilet and sink?" Gomet asked.

"Not this time." The guard turned and left.

"Give me the broom," Tam said. "This floor is atrocious." Gomet and Thadus milled around for a while until the work was finished. Another drizit scurried across the floor, seeking shelter.

"I'm beginning to hate those things. They give me the creeps," Tam said.

Tam climbed up her bunk to retrieve Ruby, but Ruby wasn't there. She checked under the pillow and blanket, but no Ruby.

"Ruby?" she called out. *'Ruby, can you hear me?'* she thought with her mind. No answer. "I've lost Ruby," she said.

"What? She's got to be here somewhere," Dram said.

Tam shook her head.

"We'll find her," he touched her shoulder. "Everybody, search your bunks," he said.

The three men searched their bunks and then they all searched the room, with no luck.

Tam ran a hand through her hair. "I liked that little dragon." She glanced down at her own feet, a sadness creeping over her. A movement under Thadus' bunk caught her eye.

"Ruby?"

'Oh, hello,' Ruby spoke telepathically. *'I was stuck in a cloth prison and couldn't get out.'*

"Where were you?" Tam asked as she scooped her up.

'I was under that bed when I got hung up in those materials.'

Tam bent down and looked under Thadus' bed. The sheets hung down to the floor. "I see what the problem is," Tam said. "Maybe we should make our beds every day so Ruby doesn't get trapped in the sheets," she suggested.

"What? Make our beds?" Gomet complained.

"It won't hurt you to be neat," Dram said.

"Yes, especially if the warden is coming. He expects this place to be clean," Thadus said.

"Well, I wonder what they have planned for us today?" Gomet said.

"Yeah, we've got more than half the day left," Thadus said.

"Well, we could read the PRMs," Tam suggested. "At least until they come back for us."

"Sounds good to me," Dram said.

She pulled the reading material from under her bunk and shared them with her cellmates. Then she climbed back up to her bunk to read to Ruby. She read 'telepathically' to Ruby.

'*That's an interesting story.*' Ruby said when she finished.

Finally, Jardan returned to their cell and opened it. "You get thirty minutes of free time outside. Let's go."

Tam put Ruby in her pouch and followed her cellmates down the hall and after riding the people mover, they headed outside.

'Nice,' Ruby spoke to Tam's mind. All of A block was enjoying the sunshine. Tam set Ruby down on a large rock.

'*Go ahead and explore, but come back to me in thirty minutes,*' Tam spoke to Ruby telepathically.

'*I don't know how to tell time,*' Ruby said.

'*Then don't let me out of your sight,*' Tam spoke again.

She watched Ruby try her wings and fly around the perimeter, when Dram approached her.

"Are you two bonding?" he asked.

"Yes, Ruby speaks to me telepathically and I speak to her that way as well."

"That's interesting," Dram said.

"She wants to meet her siblings," Tam said.

"Really? How are you going to manage that?"

"I don't know."

Ruby flew up to Tam's shoulder. '*I like it out here,*' Ruby said telepathically.

"I do, too," Tam spoke aloud. "But I'm being punished like all the others and I have to work in the mines."

'*What are you being punished for?*'

Tam realized she was speaking to a child-like creature. '*I poisoned someone and he died. I didn't mean to hurt that man,*' Tam spoke telepathically.

'*Why did you do it?*'

'*I meant to hurt someone else, not the man who took the poison.*'

'*Why did you want to poison anyone?*'

'*I felt hurt and pain for the loss of my brother. The man I meant to poison killed my brother.*' Tam thought about what she had said. She didn't want Ruby to think it was all right to poison people. *'What I did was wrong. I found out my brother was not a nice person. He was evil and hurt others and should have been punished himself. I forgave the man who killed my brother, but I still need to take my punishment.'*

'Who forgives you?' Ruby asked.

'I hope God can forgive me. My life is much better here than where I was before. I also hope that the family of the man I killed will one day forgive me. I am truly sorry for what I did,' Tam thought, and she meant it.

Ruby leaned against Tam's neck. *'Who is God?'*

'That's a good question. I think of him as my creator. The one who looks out for me.'

'Does that include dragons?'

'Yes, He created everything, so that includes you as well. He wants what is good for us, even if we suffer for a time, I think it strengthens us. At least, I hope so.'

'Did you suffer?'

'Yes. My life with my father was pure hell, so this prison is nice in comparison.'

Dram watched the interaction between Ruby and Tam. He didn't know what they were talking about, but it seemed like it was something deep. He wished he had that kind of relationship with someone. Maybe, even, Tam.

When Tam realized that he had been watching her, she explained that she and Ruby were discussing her past and talking about God.

"Would you like to see Ruby?" Tam asked him.

"Sure."

Tam placed Ruby into his hands and watched him gently pet Ruby's head.

"Why did you become a slave trader?" she asked him.

"I didn't think of it that way, really. My business partner mentioned it. He said there was a need to find good workers on some of the planets. He said people were willing to pay well for someone to locate these workers. It made sense, so we started rounding up people."

"Did you ever think about what happened to those people?"

"No. I thought of them as products. I figured they were put to work and that was the end of it."

She leaned back and looked him over. "How could you think of human beings as products? You enslaved them for the rest of their lives and uprooted families."

Dram glanced at her, then looked down. He handed Ruby back to her. "I was told the I.S.P. would search for all of them to return them to their planets and families."

"Yes, that was the intention. Some of them had only known a life of slavery, since they had been gone so long. They all need healing."

"How do you know so much about me?" Dram asked.

"I was in the I.S.P. a short time. I had to study about you. I was part of the team that was searching for those slaves."

"So, what happened to you?"

"I was really there to find Berto. I've done a lot of thinking about my situation. I lived a life as a sex slave to my father. When he discovered who killed Tedoro, he sent me after Berto. I worked on airships for a while, thinking Berto was there, but found out he was picked up by the I.S.P."

"You can repair airships?"

"Yes, but I'm not as good as Berto. In fact, Berto is the reason I am here, and for that, I'm grateful."

"Why are you grateful for being in prison?"

"This is not a prison. To me, this is freedom. I was in prison living with my father. May he never rest in Vaedran hell!" She moved to stand up, but he grabbed her arm.

"Whoa! You think this is freedom?"

"Yes, to me, it is, and I'm good with it. I've forgiven Berto and I've asked forgiveness from God. I only hope the family I've hurt can forgive me as well."

"How can you forgive Berto?"

"I let go of the pain. Besides, I learned how evil my brother was. He was becoming my father and that could not happen. You should be asking forgiveness from those you hurt, as well as from God." Tam pulled away and walked around the area with Ruby until Jardan came back to escort them to their cells.

While waiting for the evening meal, Tam glanced through her PRMs and read a story to Ruby. When she finished, Dram spoke up.

"Read another one, please."

Ruby nodded. Tam found another story and began reading it. When she finished, she realized Ruby was asleep. She sat up and glanced around the room and noticed everyone else had dozed off. She curled up under her blanket and went to sleep until she heard a loud clanging noise.

Tam jerked awake. Several guards and a strangely dressed man came down the hall. There was yelling and a commotion going on.

"What's happening?" she asked. She climbed down from her bunk and put Ruby in her pouch.

Everyone was at the cell door, waiting and listening.

"The warden is inspecting the cells," Dram whispered. "He's removing the sheets and pillows and tossing them in the hall."

"Why would he do that?" she asked.

"He's an evil man," Thadus said.

Finally, the warden was at their cell. He glanced around the cell, while the guards opened the door. Then, after inspecting the toilet, the warden looked them over, stopping in front of her. He lifted her chin, as if inspecting her. She didn't see him do that to the others. Then he reached his hand behind her and squeezed her butt. She slapped him hard in the face. He took a swing at her and she ducked, punching him hard in the groin.

"Grab her!" the warden shouted at the guards as he doubled over from her punch.

"You're my prisoner, and I'll do what I want with you," he said.

"I'm not your slave," she said.

The guard twisted her arm behind her back, causing pain to radiate throughout her shoulder. This was a new guard she had not seen before.

"Bring her!" the warden said. He turned to leave.

Dram took a swing at the guard, but the other one jumped him. Thadus and Gomet tried to stop the first guard, but the second guard stunned all three of them.

This new guard shoved her down the hall, her arm still pushed against her back. The pain was getting worse. *'Ruby are you all right?'*

'What's happening?' Ruby asked.

'Nothing good. Stay hidden.'

They arrived at Kellen's office and she watched the warden barge through the door.

"Why is she in the cell with three men?" the warden demanded.

"We have no other cells. That's the only one that had room at the time," Kellen explained.

"There's another cell with only three men in it."

"We had one prisoner that died that was in that cell," Kellen said.

The warden glared at Kellen, then at Tam. "We're taking her with us," the warden said.

"Sir, I can't let you do that," Kellen said. "Protocol."

The warden's face grew red. He walked toward the guard who still held her arm against her back and pulled the guard's weapon, turned and shot Kellen.

Tam's mouth fell open. She had no one to help her now.

"Bring her!" the warden demanded.

She watched the warden storm out of the room and they followed him. She glanced around as the guard forced her down the hall. She tried to think of a way to escape. The warden had a weapon now, but the guard did not. They came up to the ship that was parked outside the large doors. The ramp was down. The warden walked ahead. As she got closer to the door, she pressed her back into the guard and put her feet on either side of the door, walking her feet up until she could flip over the guard's head, landing on his shoulders. She let herself fall back, keeping her legs around his neck. She crossed her feet to choke him while she hung upside down. He clawed at her legs, but she tightened her legs until he buckled and fell. She jumped away and ran as fast and as far as she could.

All she could hear was shouting until she could get to the mountains. There weren't too many places to hide since it was rocky without any shrubs or trees. It was mere minutes before the ship flew over the mountains. By then, she was well hidden in a crevasse. Ruby stood guard.

'The ship is gone, Tam. It went straight up. I don't see it anymore.'

She was afraid they would come back. If the warden was gone, she would be safe, wouldn't she? She had no way to survive out here on her own. Besides, things could get worse if the warden found her. *'I'm going back, Ruby. I felt safer inside than I feel out here.'*

She slipped back to the entrance and pulled on the doors. They weren't locked. She ran down the hall to Kellen's office. There was a commotion there. She searched the room for the warden and his guards, but they weren't there.

"Is Kellen all right?" she asked. The guards turned to her.

"He was stunned. He'll be fine shortly. How did you get out of your cell?"

"The warden tried to take me with him. I escaped. Please don't make me go with the warden. Please!"

One of the guards took her back to her cell. "The warden will be back, only the next time, he won't be so nice to you."

"He wasn't nice to me this time, either."

~

"Why didn't you escape?" Dram asked.

"Where would I go?"

"Anywhere but here," Thadus said.

"They searched for me, so I hid until they were gone. I don't have survival skills."

"Sure, you do. You'd figure things out as you went," Dram said.

"Maybe. But I feel safe here."

He poked her chest with his finger. "The next time you escape, don't come back. You can make it out there. Prison is no place for a woman."

She thought about what Dram had said. But now they were all sleeping on old mattresses without sheets and pillows. She liked things the way they were before the warden showed up.

~

"Kellen! What's happened to you?" Marla asked. She moved to rub his back.

Kellen slumped at his desk, his head resting on his arms. He forced himself up at hearing Marla's voice.

"That damn warden came in here, stripping all the bedding off the beds. Then he tried to take our female prisoner with him. Said she was *his* prisoner and he could do what he wanted with her. He tried to take her with him but she escaped. He'll be back and it won't be good for any of us."

"We told him we would be making changes. I'll report this to the committee. That man should not be allowed to stay," Marla said.

Later, Tam and Ruby were snuggled in bed. *'That was some adventure we had today, Ruby.'*

'I agree with Dram. We should escape again.'

'We can't now. We're locked in this place.'

'Next time, we'll make it.'

'What makes you think there will be a next time?'

'That bad man will come back and we will escape.'

Dram thought about what Tam had said earlier about feeling safe here. He ran his hand through his hair. His hair had grown long and shaggy. He couldn't remember the last time he had his hair cut. All three of the men had shaggy hair. They looked rough around the edges. He was glad none of the men in the Vaedra system grew hair on their faces, like his son Adam had. When he saw Adam the last time, his face looked bushy. It was something he inherited from his Earthen mother.

The thought of Emma made him sad. He was sorry he left her on Earth, but she refused to come with him. He should have taken her anyway. If he had, he wouldn't have become a slave-trader, and she would be alive today. But he couldn't imagine any other lifestyle he was suited for, other than slave-trading. He could have helped raise Adam. He smiled at the thought. Adam turned out pretty good after all. He was a lot like Emma. He had no ill feelings about the boy, even though he was the one who captured him.

Then the thought of Dirk crossed his mind. He wasn't sorry for killing Dirk since he was the one responsible for the death of Emma and her husband, leaving Adam an orphan. He thought about all the other people he had sold into slavery. Maybe he should be sorry about them. Twenty-five anos of slave-trading added up to a lot of people. If they had only been used for manual labor, then that wasn't so bad.

Then he wondered what happened to the young girls and women. He had never thought about their fates before. Could they have been used as sex slaves, like Tam had? And how could her own father do that to her? He fisted his hands. If his cellmates hadn't already killed him, he would have done it himself.

And that warden was about to use Tam as his own private sex slave. He wondered if the girls and women he had sold into slavery would have reacted like Tam. He smiled at the thought of her escaping. She did have survival skills. She just didn't realize it.

He tossed and turned from all the thoughts racing through his mind. It was a long time before he could drift off to sleep.

The next day, things went back to normal as far as routines go. Tam, Thadus, and the others worked the gems out of the rock. Ruby crawled around a ledge while Tam chiseled the gems loose. In between strikes, Tam heard Ruby shriek.

"What is it, Ruby?" she asked.

'Danger!'

Tam felt a slight tremor. She pushed off from the wall and grabbed Ruby off her ledge. "Thadus! Did you feel that?"

"Yes! Bronin! Get us down!"

Bronin worked feverishly, lowering all the harnesses when another tremor occurred. This time it was harder. Tam saw two men drop fifty feet quickly.

'Hang on, Ruby!' She felt her harness drop rapidly and rolled when she landed. Thadus wasn't as lucky. He hit hard and didn't roll. Tam ran toward him when some large rocks fell nearby.

"Thadus! Thadus! Talk to me," Tam shouted. She covered his body with hers when the ground trembled again, dislodging more rocks.

"Let's go!" Bronin shouted.

Two men ran past Tam but more heavy rocks fell between them and Bronin. Bronin had left them all behind.

"I think Thadus is alive. Can you help me with him?" she asked the two men. The three of them were able to get Thadus in a sitting position. He was still groggy.

"Where are the others?" Tam asked.

"They didn't make it," one of the men said.

There had been four more men that worked this section of the mine. "None of them?" she asked.

"A boulder crushed them," the other one answered.

"How can we get out?" Tam asked.

"The only way out is the people mover," the first one said.

"We'll have to climb over those boulders," Tam said. "Can you make it, Thadus?"

"I don't feel right," he said.

"Gomet!" Dram called out. He found his way to the vat of liquid tulin, where he had last seen Gomet. He was pinned under the heavy vat. Dram checked for a pulse but found none. The ground shook again.

"Anybody here?" Dram shouted. A couple men ran toward him.

"There's no one else alive down here. Where's the guard?"

"I haven't seen him," Dram said.

"Let's head to the people mover," one of the men said.

"I tried. You need the guard's badge to call it down."

"We're stuck here?" one of them asked.

"Calm down. There are hundreds of men trapped on different levels. They would have to get them out first since we're on the bottom level," Dram said. "We've got to find another way. Spread out and see if you can feel any air shafts. We'll work from there." The three men spread out, feeling for air shafts and hoping to find another way to escape.

~

'Ruby, can you find us a way out?'

'I'll see what I can find.'

Tam turned Ruby loose, watching her make her way up the fallen rocks. Tam glanced at Thadus and saw the color drain from his face. "Thadus! Don't you die on me!" she said. She felt for his pulse but found none. "No!"

One of the men came toward her. "What is it?"

"Check his pulse, please!" she pleaded.

He touched Thadus' neck, then shook his head. "I'm sorry."

"Yeah, me, too. He was one of my cellmates."

Tam heard some squeaking noise. She stood and tried to locate the sound. "Ruby? Where are you?"

'I found an opening.' Ruby flew to Tam's shoulder. 'It's up there.' Ruby pointed with her wing.

Tam glanced around and found her harness. It was still attached to the rocks above. "Grab your harness and start climbing," she said.

The three of them used the harnesses as ropes and pulled and climbed their way up the rocks.

Ruby flew off Tam's shoulder and landed on a ledge. *'In here.'*

When Tam reached the ledge, she felt a cool breeze through the cracks. She pulled her tools out of her pouch and started chiseling at the rocks. When the two men joined her, they were able to break more of the rock fragments away, making an opening. The three of them used their hammers and chisels to create a line down the boulder, shattering a large portion. Tam tried to squeeze through the opening.

"I still can't get through, but I can feel the cool air flowing in beyond the boulder."

The three of them continued working their tools on the boulder until another large chunk fell away. One of the men squeezed through. He reached his hand out to pull Tam through. Finally, the last man squeezed through.

Ruby clung to Tam's shoulder. This part of the cave was black. Ruby made a barking noise and shot out a small flame.

"Thank you, Ruby. I didn't know you could do that."

'I didn't either. This way.'

The three of them crawled on hands and knees toward the breeze, while Ruby walked ahead. Every now and then, she barked out a light so they could see where they were.

'It feels like we are going up,' she spoke to Ruby.

'We are. It's not far now.'

"I smell fresh air," Tam said.

"Me, too," one of the men said.

When they reached the opening, it was too small for the men to fit through.

"Use your tools," Tam said. "We've come this far. You can't stop now."

The men used their hammers and beat the rock. "It's soft. We won't need the chisels," one of them said.

Finally, the bigger man pushed through the opening. Tam and the other man followed.

"Careful. We're on a peak," the big one said.

"How are we going to get down? It's too steep," the other man said.

"Without our ropes, we're stuck up here," Tam said. Ruby squeaked.

'Can you help us, Ruby? Can you find us a way down?"

'Yes, I can do that!' she squeaked again. Ruby flew down the mountain.

chapter five

AFTER LONG MINUTES of searching for an opening with no luck, Dram had an idea. He climbed back down to where he left his plasma drill. He aimed it at a rock. Nothing came out, but it left a large hole. He continued drilling in a wider area.

"Grab your plasma drills. If we take turns drilling holes, the plasma can recharge." The two men found their drills and the three of them took turns making the hole deeper as they went up the interior of the mountain. The plasma drills grew heavy with each passing hour, but they made their way further up the mountain until a point of light hit Dram in the eyes.

"I think we've found a way out," Dram said. He blasted once more and a gaping hole revealed the landscape of where they ate the mid-day meals. Standing at the edge of freedom, he saw there was a sheer drop of over a hundred keks, with no one in sight.

~

"Kellen, all the levels are blocked off by the quake.

Bronin hasn't reported in and neither have Endor, Jael, Kyle or Kobe," Jardan said.

"Get the drones out on each level and see what they turn up," Kellen said.

"We're going to need a rescue squad," Jardan said.

"I've already called it in. All the back-up guards are on alert and Marla has notified the committee as well as the warden."

"I sure as hell hope the warden doesn't show up. That's all we need," Jardan said. He left the office and headed for the drone controls in the hall. He turned on each drone on each level of the mine. He programmed them to search for life signs. He was responsible for all the guards. He hoped they all survived. He checked the panel beside the controls and monitored each level. On the lowest level, where they mined for tulin, the drone found three lifeless bodies, but it beeped at the people mover.

"I've got someone on level one trapped inside the people mover. It's got to be Kobe and possibly some prisoner," Jardan spoke into his communicator.

"Got it," Kellen said.

Jardan watched the drone on the second level. It showed at least four lifeless bodies. He glanced at the third level, where there were more miners. The drone began beeping. "I see at least ten survivors on level three," Jardan said.

"Got it. We'll start the search there and work down to the people mover on level one," Kellen said.

On level four, the drone picked up multiple bodies, all alive, but not moving. "I have life on level four. It appears to be six people with possible injuries," Jardan said.

The drones on levels five and six picked up twenty people on each. "It looks like more survivors on levels five and six," Jardan said.

"The teams are arriving as we speak. Keep monitoring the drones and keep me apprised of the situation," Kellen said.

"Will do," Jardan responded.

Dram used the plasma drill a few more times, making small holes angling down the mountain.

"What are you doing?" Keo asked him.

"I'm making some handholds so we can climb down. I'm not staying in this mine another night," Dram said.

"If these drills weren't so heavy, we could carry them with us down the mountain," Madda said.

"Give me your shirt," Dram demanded.

"Why?" Madda asked.

"I'll make a strap to carry my plasma drill so I can make handholds all the way down the mountain."

Madda removed his shirt, but Dram only used the long sleeves to make a strap. He returned what was left of the shirt to Madda.

"I'll go first. Give me a few minutes before following and make sure to use all the handholds," Dram said.

He angled his plasma drill once more and made a few more handholds before gingerly stepping into the first one. The plasma drill was over his shoulder. The weight of the drill pulled him away from the mountain with each step. He had to be careful. While using the drill from the safety of the cave they created, it made deep holes to grab onto. When he was near the last hold, he angled the drill again and made three more holes in the rock surface. He moved down slowly. Another three holes and he was on the ground. He glanced around. Still no sign of people, but he heard a lot of noise coming from the other side of the mountain. It must be the rescue equipment. They would have to drill down into the mountain, creating a large shaft to get everyone out.

Tam took her hammer and smashed it into the rock. The two men followed suit and they created some handholds to get down to a narrow path that Ruby alerted them to. It was slow and tedious, but they managed to get to the narrow path.

"Where did you find that dragon?" Kragg asked her.

"I found her after Thadus and I pulled that geode out. Her nest was behind it," Tam said.

"Are you speaking with her telepathically?" Cannon asked.

"Yes. She can't speak just yet because her vocal cords aren't developed."

After a couple hours, they managed to get to the bottom of the mountain. "I think we should wait until nightfall and cross over to the other side of the compound," Kragg said.

"Don't you remember the layout of this place?" Tam asked.

"What do you mean?" Cannon asked.

"When I flew into this place, that side was where all the single guards live. We're going to have to cross this mountain."

The three of them looked up at the tall, craggy mountains.

Jardan had been watching the drone on the bottom level, when it stopped. It shown the light up and down a surface that just didn't look right. He zoomed in on the drone's camera. It appeared to be a hole. Jardan hit the command button to follow the hole to where it led. It looked more like a tunnel as he watched. He finally saw movement, then the drone went dead. He hit all the buttons, but the drone was down.

"Kellen, I think the drone on level one picked up some movement, but it went dead. No live bodies were in the main shaft, but the movement came from some tunnel I've never seen before."

"Got it. I've got everyone working on rescue efforts. I can't spare anyone to search outside."

"I can go, if you want. I don't see anything new on these drone screens since my last report."

"Good. Let me know if we have any survivors," Kellen said.

Jardan headed to the equipment room to locate another drone. He couldn't get any out of the mines, but he thought there was one spare in the equipment room.

By the time Madda and Keo made it to the bottom, it had gotten dark. "We'll have to cross in front of the main doors to get to the mountains," Dram said.

"Why don't we go this way?" Keo pointed to the left.

"The guards live out there. We must go over the mountains," Dram said.

"Yes, and we better hurry. I just took out a drone in that tunnel we created."

"Damn!" Dram moved out to the edge of the rock face, checking for anything moving. "I think we're clear, let's go."

He hunched over and ran past the main doors, which were closed. A large piece of equipment drilled into the rock from the top, trying to create a shaft to locate the prisoners.

The three of them managed to get to the mountains on the other side of the equipment.

"This side looks just as steep as the other side," Keo said.

"You're right. If we don't find a good place to start up, we'll have to make our way up with the plasma drill," Dram said.

"Won't they see the plasma light?" Madda asked.

"Probably, so we need to find another way up," Dram said.

The three of them walked along the bottom of the mountain for almost an hour. Finally, Dram found what he was looking for. "An animal path," he said.

"I wonder what kind of animal lives in the mountains," Madda said.

Dram climbed up the shorter rocks and found the narrow path. Keo and Madda followed. It was slow going for a while.

Tam, Kragg and Cannon continued their climb up the mountain. Ruby rested on Tam's shoulder. "I don't know about you two, but I'm getting tired," Tam said.

"Let's find a spot and sleep for the night," Kragg said.

"Yeah, some place hidden, like that cave over there," Cannon said. The three of them headed to the cave, but Tam hesitated.

"Do you smell that?" Tam asked.

"Smell what?" Kragg said.

"I smell it, too." Cannon said.

"Something dead. Let's not go in there," Tam said.

'It smells like food,' Ruby said. *'Let me check.'*

'Ruby, be careful,' Tam spoke with her mind. Ruby flew off her shoulder and flew into the cave.

She heard Ruby bark and then saw her flame light up a portion of the cave. A cave with a dragon in it.

"Did you see that?" Kragg asked.

"Yes." Tam backed into Kragg. Kragg backed up, pulling Tam with him. Tam glanced over her shoulder and Cannon was even farther back than they were.

'Ruby? Are you all right?'

Ruby flew back to Tam. *'I'm fine. My new friend, Tallie, said we can stay in the cave with her tonight. Tomorrow, she will take us over the mountain.'*

"Uh, guys? Ruby's new friend will let us stay the night in her cave. Tomorrow, she'll take us over the mountain."

"How do you know that? Cannon asked.

"Because Ruby spoke to her."

"How do you know she won't try to eat us?" Kragg asked.

"Because I've eaten humans and they are too salty," Tallie said.

Tam glanced at Kragg.

Tallie pulled her half-eaten animal to her and moved closer to the far wall. "You can have that side," Tallie said.

"Thank you," Tam said. She moved into the cave. Kragg and Cannon followed behind her. The three of them sat together against the opposite wall from Tallie.

Cannon's stomach growled and then Tam's. They had worked hard all day trying to get free and climbing this mountain. She was very thirsty. "Is there a source of water nearby?" Tam asked.

"In the back of the cave is a waterfall. Help yourself," Tallie said.

Tam headed to the back of the cave. There was no light, but she could hear the water. She felt something on her shoulder. "Ruby! I need your light," she said. Ruby barked out a flame, and Tam could see where the waterfall was. She reached out and cupped her hands. She drank and drank until she felt full. She heard movement behind her.

"Where's the water?" Kragg asked.

Ruby barked out her flame once more and Tam watched Kragg and Cannon drink from the life-giving water.

"Oh, that's good," Kragg said.

"Yes. We're going to have to find something to eat tonight," Cannon said.

"It's too dark to hunt. I think we'll have to search for something in the morning," Tam said.

"I hope I can make it till morning," Cannon said.

"We don't have a choice, Cannon," Kragg said. They returned to their original spots and fell asleep beside each other.

Jardan tracked the drone he sent out at dusk. He had made large circular patterns searching close and moving out. He had to return to the panel inside to check for survivors for Kellen. Once again, he looked over the different levels. The one he couldn't check any more was the first level, where Dram and a few men worked the tulin mines. He couldn't be sure, but someone dug out that tunnel and someone destroyed the drone. How many, he wasn't sure because the drone didn't show more than three casualties. There were only six men and a guard on that level. Did the guard survive?

An alarm sounded. Jardan checked the panel again. The large drill reached the level six mine. He could see ropes drop down into the mine with light flooding the area. First people down were healers and rescuers, checking for survivors. Then he felt the tremors.

"Not again." Jardan mumbled. He checked the panels. More rocks had fallen in the second and third levels. "Did you feel that, Kellen?"

"Yes, I did. What have you got for me?"

"If they keep drilling in the same spot, they will reach the fifth level. There are more survivors there, but the tremors are affecting the lowest levels."

"Anything on the drone you sent out?" Kellen asked.

"Nothing. The light is dim. I can call it back and send it out again in the morning."

"Go ahead. I'm sending your replacement so you can get some rest.

Marla had been working on prison reform for anos. This was a newer prison but it had not been renovated for the new updates. She had the agreement of the committee and the supervisors in the court system as well as the counselors for all the planets. These new updates were to be made in all the prisons on each planet. Plumaris was the place everyone ended up once they received their sentences. There were three large prisons on Plumaris and one warden. Did he remove the bedding from all the prisons? And had he tried to remove prisoners himself for his own personal use? She would get to the bottom of this. Marla headed her ship to the other prisons for inspection.

Once the prisoners were checked for injuries, they were returned to their cells and food was brought to them. After what they had gone through, Kellen had all the bedding cleaned and returned to each of the prisoners. He wasn't going to let the warden undo the good work Marla had put into this prison reform. He saw the differences in the attitudes. What she was trying to do was give them back their dignity.

⸾

"Over there!" Dram pointed.

"I see it," Keo said.

"What is it?" Madda asked.

"Duck!" Dram flattened himself on the trail. Keo and Madda did the same. "It's a transport. I hope they didn't see us."

Dram waited for a while before checking again. "I think they're gone. We need to find something to eat."

"I haven't seen anything that passes for food around here," Keo said.

"We've been on an eeya's trail for a while now," Dram said. Without any tools, Dram had to figure out a way to capture an eeya. Would a plasma drill kill it? Would it still be edible? And how were they going to cook it? He glanced at the rocks around him. He needed a knife. He took a small rock and bashed it against other rocks, splintering pieces of the hard surface. He picked up the pieces and inspected them. These will have to do.

"What are you doing?" Madda asked.

"Surviving."

"By breaking rocks?" Keo asked.

"I made a weapon."

"Why?" Keo asked.

"You want to eat, don't you?"

"Sure," Keo said.

"Start gathering wood for a fire," Dram said.

While Keo and Madda looked for wood, Dram slipped over the edge of the ridge. He got as close as he could before aiming at and shooting the eeya. Its head was bashed in from the plasma drill. He took the splintered rocks and cut through the neck of the eeya, removing the head. Then, he carefully skinned the eeya the best he could. He cut through the body cavity, pulling out the guts. He cut strips of skin to tie the legs together for cooking. Then, heaving the carcass over one shoulder, and the plasma drill over the other, he climbed back up to where Keo and Madda were.

"Wow, what's that?" Keo asked.

"Evening meal," Dram said.

"That's going to take a while to cook, won't it?" Madda asked.

"Yes, it will, unless you want to eat it raw."

"No thanks," Keo said.

"Hold this," Dram said. He handed Madda the eeya. "I've got to rig up something to cook it on." He found the items he needed and prepared a makeshift spit for the carcass.

"We'll have to take turns rotating the meat so it will cook through," Dram said.

"How do you know what you're doing?" Madda asked.

Dram recalled how he landed on Earth long ago and had to figure out how to survive until he met Emma. Then, when he was back on Meta, he and Timna had to figure out how to build a slave-trading business on a desolate moon. "If you want to stay out of prison, you've got to learn how to survive."

Tam got a whiff of something in the air. Something burning? No. It was more like something cooking. She sat up and opened her eyes. *'Do you smell that, Ruby?'*

'Yes. It smells like food.'

'It certainly does.' Tam's stomach growled at the smell.

She glanced at Kragg and Cannon. Cannon opened his eyes and glanced at her. "I smell something cooking," he whispered.

Kragg opened his eyes and so did Tallie. Tallie stretched. "I think I'll go investigate this smell," she said. "Come, Ruby. I'll teach you how to hunt."

Ruby flew off with Tallie.

Kragg waited until they were alone. "Do you trust the dragon?" he asked.

"We don't have a choice. I just hope that's not the guards out there, cooking a meal," Tam said.

Dram took his place beside the spit and rotated the meat. He glanced up at the dark sky.

"What is it?" Madda asked.

"I thought I saw something," Dram said.

"A drone?" Keo sat up.

"No, something much bigger."

"A ship?" Madda asked.

"What the Vaedran hell is that?" Keo asked. He fell off the rock he had been sitting on. Madda backed up and tripped over Keo while something huge landed near their fire. Dram noticed a familiar shape jump off the dragon. "Ruby? Is that you?" Dram asked. He knelt and held out his hand. Ruby came to him and squeaked. "Is Tam with you? Is she all right?"

Ruby squeaked then flew off his hand and landed near the dragon. It appeared they were communicating telepathically.

"Hello," Dram said.

Madda and Keo jumped to their feet and stood behind Dram.

"Ruby tells me you are a friend to Tam," the dragon spoke.

"Yes. We were cellmates until the quake. Is she all right?"

"She and her two companions are fine. You smell like my favorite food."

"I, uh, got blood on my shirt. I left a pile of guts down there," he pointed. "You're welcome to that and some of this meat when it's finished cooking."

The dragon nodded. "Come Ruby." The dragon flew over the ridge with Ruby following her.

"What just happened?" Keo asked.

"My cellmate found the tiny dragon while mining. She kept her a secret from the guards. She must be alive somewhere on this mountain."

"I didn't know dragons could talk," Madda said.

The dragon returned with Ruby. "I can help you with your

meat if you're willing to share with the others," the dragon said.

"How?" Dram asked.

Tallie belched out a flame and finished cooking the meat.

"Thank you. I'm Dram," he said.

"I'm Tallie. I will take you to my cave where the others are and you'll be safe."

"Can we eat first?" Madda asked.

"Tam and her companions are hungry, too." Tallie lowered her head. "Climb onto my back and I'll take you there."

Dram grabbed the meat off the spit and kicked dirt over the fire to put it out. He climbed onto Tallie's back, gingerly holding the hot carcass. Madda and Keo joined him on Tallie's back.

"Hang on," she said.

chapter six

THE DRAGON LANDED at the mouth of a cave. Ruby had clung to Dram's shoulder. His heart hitched at the sight of Tam. She looked tired and worn, but just seeing her made his heart lighten. Ruby flew off his shoulder and landed on Tam. He climbed down from Tallie's back. He had the plasma drill over one shoulder and the meat in the other hand.

Before he could reach Tam, he heard shouting. Madda took a swing at a man sitting next to Tam. Tam ducked out of the way and the man raised his arms in self-defense. As he shifted the meat onto his shoulder, he saw Tallie swing around and eat Madda whole.

"Tallie! I thought you didn't eat people?" Tam yelled.

"Hmm. No, I said humans were salty. I won't have angry people in my cave." Tallie licked her lips and glanced at the man Madda hit. He jumped up and stood behind Tam. Another man joined him.

"Uh, anyone else hungry?" Dram asked. He offered the eeya carcass to Keo.

"Dram!" Tam ran toward him. Ruby flew off her shoulder as Dram embraced her. She felt good in his arms and he realized she held him as tight as he held her. "I'm glad you made it out alive," he said.

She pulled away slightly. "Thadus didn't make it," she said.

He pulled her close again. "Neither did Gomet." He walked her back to the group. They shared the meat among themselves until they were full and gave the rest to Tallie and Ruby.

The five of them hunkered down and slept against the cave wall, trying to stay warm. The temperature had dropped since the sun went down.

The next morning, Dram awoke with Tam's arm across his chest. He smiled at the thought of her touch. Maybe she was growing fond of him. It had been so long since he had a woman in his arms. Last night gave him hope that maybe he had a chance of having a relationship with her.

A movement to his left got his attention. It was Tallie, stretching. Now that it was daylight, he could see how sharp her teeth were. This reminded him how one minute there were three of them and the next, there were two.

He caught Tam glancing over his head and he swung around. There, in the distance, was a drone. "Damn!" He scrambled to his feet and so did Tam. They woke the others.

"Get behind me," Tallie said.

The small group scrambled behind Tallie's body and waited.

Dram heard Tallie cough and a flame shot out at the drone, melting it instantly. Tallie had been an asset to them from the beginning. He glanced around the area. "Where's Ruby?" he asked.

He heard a shrieking noise and saw Ruby land on Tam's shoulder.

"I think you're getting bigger, Ruby," Tam said.

"I am," Ruby shrieked out.

"Ruby! Those were your first words!" Tam kissed the side of Ruby's face.

Tallie slowly stretched. "They will be back," she said. "We may as well head out."

The five of them climbed on Tallie's back. She flew over the mountain range until she reached a nice, grassy area with a nearby forest.

"This will do nicely," Dram said.

"I often hunt here. The eeya are plentiful, as well as smaller creatures," she said.

"Creatures? What kind of creatures?" Cannon asked.

"Hopping things and flying things," Tallie said.

When everyone had climbed down from Tallie's back, Dram walked up to her. "Thank you, Tallie, for helping us. I appreciate your kindness."

Tallie nodded. "Kindness to dragons will not go un-rewarded," Tallie said.

Tam joined him and touched the side of Tallie's face. "Thank you, Tallie."

"You have protected my young one. For that I am grateful. I have not found any of my other hatchlings."

"Ruby is your hatchling?" Tam asked.

"Yes. I made the nest in your mountain to protect them, but I have not seen any of them leave the mountain." Tallie turned toward Ruby. "Come Ruby. I will teach you how to survive," Tallie said.

"Oh, Ruby, I'm going to miss you," Tam said.

"Me too," Ruby squeaked.

"Are there any others like you?" Dram asked.

"My mate and I were shot at. He was hit, but I don't know if he made it. I found the opening in the mountain and made my nest there. After laying my eggs, I sealed up the area the best I could, to keep the eggs safe. We are the last dragons on Plumaris."

"Don't forget me, Ruby," Tam said. She kissed Ruby's

forehead. Ruby flew to Tallie and landed on her back. Dram stood beside Tam and watched the two dragons fly away. Tam hung her head. "I loved that little dragon," she said.

Dram ran his hand across her back. "Those drones are capable of picking up our heat signatures."

Tam glanced up at him. "There's no way to escape," she said.

"I'm not giving up without a fight," Dram said.

Cannon walked up to them. "Good riddance, I say."

"What?" Tam grabbed Cannon's shirt and pulled him close, with one hand. The other hand, she balled into a fist.

Dram put his hand on her shoulder. "Uh, Tam, remember the last person who showed anger in front of Tallie?"

Tam glanced up at the sky. Tallie was already gone.

"I meant the big dragon, not your pet," Cannon said.

Tam let go of Cannon's shirt.

"Yeah, she could have turned on all of us at some point," Keo said.

"What was your problem with Madda?" Dram asked. He glared at Cannon.

"He had been angry at me for a while. We had been cell-mates. Madda accused me of taking something of his but I didn't. Madda had always been a bully. He took what he wanted whenever he wanted," Cannon explained.

Kragg glanced around the area. "I think we should split up. They will be able to track us easier if we're together. And I don't trust that warden. When he wants something, he doesn't stop until he gets it."

Tam glanced at Dram. "I'm with you," she said.

"Good luck," Dram called out. He took Tam by the hand and headed into the woods. Once they were under cover of the trees, he glanced back at the sky. "They will probably send a ship this next time," he said.

"What do we do first? Find shelter or find food?" Tam asked.

"We find shelter," he said.

"What is that you're carrying?" Tam asked.

"My plasma drill. It will come in handy if we can find shelter in a cave."

"Is it heavy?"

"Yes. It's how we escaped. The three of us each had one, but I'm the only one who kept his. We were able to make a tunnel with them."

"We escaped with our chisels and hammers," Tam said. She raised her hand to show him her tools.

"Hang on to them. We may need them later."

The two of them walked for hours until they heard a strange noise. "What is that?" Tam asked.

"It sounds like a waterfall. I've got an idea," he said. He took her hand and led her through the woods to the sound.

He caught Tam looking over her shoulder several times. "What are you looking for?" he asked.

"I was making sure no one followed us," she said.

"If they're smart, they won't, otherwise, what's the point of splitting up?"

"True. Before it gets much later, do you think we should make some weapons for hunting? I'm getting hungry," she said.

He glanced around and picked up a couple long branches off the forest floor. He pulled out his stones and worked on the smaller branches until he had a smoother looking stick. Then, he sharpened the end to make a point. "Here you go," he said. He handed the shorter stick to Tam. Then he worked on the longer stick until it was ready.

"All we need now is to find something to eat," he said.

They walked on until they came across a creek. They followed it on until it became a river. The sound they heard earlier got louder. Finally, he saw the waterfall. Hopefully there was a cave or something like it behind the falls.

He carefully climbed up the slippery rocks behind the falls

and found a rock wall. Dram slipped the plasma drill off his shoulder and shot several times at the wall, turning it into a grotto. He waited a few moments to let the drill re-charge and tried again. This time, he had turned the grotto into a small cave, big enough for the two of them. He set the drill into the cave and carefully climbed back out.

When he got to the riverbank, he found Tam, holding the weapon he had made, full of pesca.

"I've got our evening meal if you have a way to make a fire," Tam said.

Dram created a fire from sparking the stones together. Tam helped gather wood for the fire while Dram put the pesca onto another stick he propped up over the fire. While the pesca cooked, Dram gathered some large leaves. "We'll use these to sleep on," he said.

They feasted on the pesca. "This was good, but I'll have to learn how to cook with minimal equipment," Tam said.

"It's a learning experience for both of us," Dram said. Once they were done, he watched Tam lick her fingers clean.

"I'm tempted to jump in the river and cleanse myself," Tam said.

"I wouldn't do that now, if I were you," he said.

"Why not?"

"Because the temperature will be dropping soon and we have no blankets."

"Good point."

Dram put out the fire by drenching it with water. Then he helped Tam climb up behind the waterfall.

"This is cozy," she said.

Dram threw the large leaves across the damp floor of the small cave, then climbed inside. "Here, you sleep on the inside and I'll take the outside," he said.

Tam lay down on the leaf mat and Dram lay next to her. "I think we'll be safe from the drones tonight. I don't think they will pick up our heat signatures with the rocks and waterfall surrounding us."

"How did you learn how to do all this?" she asked him.

"I crash landed on Earth when my ship broke down. I found myself in a wooded area and had to figure out how to survive. That's where I met Emma. She lived nearby in a cabin with her parents. I fell in love with her."

"How did that feel?"

"Love?"

"Yes."

"You've never been in love?"

"No."

He studied her. She looked serious. "Your heart does flip flops in your chest. You feel mariposas in your stomach when the person is around you. Sometimes you do and say stupid things because you're not thinking straight, and you think about that person all the time when they aren't with you."

She gave him a sideways glance and smiled.

"What?" he asked.

"I can't imagine you doing stupid things," she said.

"Well, I did. I took her for my mate. She helped me find parts for my communicator so I could call out for help. When I was able to get a salvage ship to pick me up, she refused to go with me."

"You left her there?" she asked.

"Yes, and she was with child."

"If you loved her, how could you do that? Didn't you think about staying with her?"

"The salvage ship was waiting on me. I didn't have time to think about it."

"What about the child?"

"He's your age now," he said.

"How do you know that?"

"He's the reason I'm...I was in prison."

"No. You were in prison for slave-trading. He may have helped capture you, but you did that to yourself."

He studied her again. "You're right. I did that to myself. If I had stayed with her, I would never have gotten into slave-trading." He lay back on the leaf mat, his arms behind his head.

He thought about how she took another mate who raised Adam. Adam turned out to be a good kid after all. Dram wasn't cut out to be a father.

"What would you have done with your life if you had stayed with her?" Tam asked.

"I don't know, maybe something with communications equipment. I worked on communications on Meta."

"Meta? That's where we trained for the I.S.P. They've turned it into a base for new recruits."

"That was *my* base, my headquarters."

"Yes. It was impressive. Maybe you'll get to do that again one day." She turned against the rock wall and went to sleep.

He sat up and stared at her back. "Goodnight Tam."

"Goodnight," she said without turning over.

He ran his hand through his tangled hair. It was now down to his shoulders. He wasn't used to having hair this long and it bothered him. Tam's once short and spiky hair had grown out as well, but his hair was longer than hers. He lay back down and tried to sleep. All he could think about was the moment he saw Tam and realized she was still alive. He felt the mariposas in his stomach. And when he and Tam had embraced, his heart did flip flops in his chest. Lying beside her and not touching her, made it difficult to sleep.

The next morning, after taking care of his bodily needs, Dram heard a noise in the woods. The sound was barely audible above the noise of the waterfall. He stood quietly, straining to make out the sound. Something was moving through the woods at a fast pace. Was it an animal?

He slipped behind the falls and woke Tam. He motioned for her to be quiet. Together, they sat, peering from behind the falls and waited. Then, he heard the splash of water. He held his breath. A hand reached through the falls, grabbing the rock ledge they sat on. He and Tam stood up to a crouch in their alcove-type cave. Cannon's head poked through the water.

"Well, well. This looks cozy. Mind if I join you?" Cannon said.

"There isn't enough room," Dram said.

"There's a drone out there trying to find us," Cannon said.

Dram pulled Tam back down into a sitting position, leaving barely enough room for Cannon to stand on the ledge.

"How long have you two been here?" Cannon whispered.

"Just last night," Dram whispered back.

"Where are the other two?" Tam whispered.

"We got separated when we saw the drone. We all took off in different directions," Cannon whispered.

"How long ago did you see it?" Dram whispered.

"A couple hours," Cannon whispered.

"Why did you jump into the river?" Tam asked.

"To lower my body temperature, but now I'm cold."

Dram and Tam sat behind the falls for a couple hours, listening for the sound of a drone and watching Cannon. Something about Cannon just didn't sit right with him. Tam stirred next to him and whispered into his ear. Her breath gave him shivers he hadn't expected.

"I've got to relieve myself." She crawled out from behind the falls and peered around. Then she stepped out from behind their safe place.

~

Marla, Denton, Mantooth, and Admiral Whitson sat at the table with the warden. Kellen stood off to the side.

The warden slammed his fist on the table. "I want those criminals found and killed."

"You can't do that," Whitson said.

"I can and I will," the warden shouted. He stood up and turned to leave the table, but Kellen shoved him back into his seat.

"I've given this committee a list of things you've done around here that goes against the inmates' rights," Kellen said.

The warden glared at him.

"You removed all the things the committee had put into place to give the inmates some dignity. They were producing more minerals and gems because of the new additions and implementations. Since you took everything away, the morale has fallen drastically," Kellen said.

"They don't deserve any of that," the warden said.

"I agree," Mantooth said.

Marla, Denton, and the Admiral glared at Mantooth. "Maybe it's time we removed you from the committee," the Admiral said.

"I second that," Marla said.

"All in favor?" Admiral Whitson said. Marla, Denton, and Whitson raised their hands.

"You may leave the room," the Admiral said to Mantooth. Mantooth stood up and stormed out of the room.

"We are this close to removing you," Whitson said. He held two fingers together with barely any space between them.

"You can't remove me! I was appointed by the Council of Nations," the warden said.

"A meeting of the Council is coming up this moon cycle and I will report to them on your behavior with this prison system. Perhaps we need a different person at each location," Admiral Whitson said.

"Yes, someone who believes in the rights of all humans. Even though they may be incarcerated, they still have rights," Marla said.

"I need more guards to help in the search and capture of any escapees," Kellen said. "I've got everyone working on rescuing those on level three and we have two more levels to go. All the guards I have are working day and night."

"I will return with another ship and more guards to help in rescue efforts as well as capturing the escapees. How many escapees do you think you have?" the warden asked.

"Only one was seen escaping from level six. We haven't gotten to that level yet to determine survivors. Another drone was destroyed by fire," Kellen said.

"Fire? How is that possible?" the warden asked.

"It was early morning in the mountains. We searched for the escapee, but what we saw was hard to determine. The lighting was bad, but the object was dark and large and the next thing was a fire, then the drone was destroyed," Kellen said.

"I will bring more drones and guards to help in your efforts." The warden stood. "If you don't mind, I have work to do." The warden left the room.

"We need to move quickly on his replacement," Denton said.

"I agree. I don't trust that man," Marla said.

"After what he tried to do to our female inmate, makes him no better than the criminals we have here," Kellen said.

chapter seven

"WHATEVER WE DO, we need to do it now," Tam whispered.

"I agree. They may still be looking for survivors and not escapees," Dram said.

"What? You don't believe me about the drone?" Cannon asked.

"I'm not sure what I believe," Dram said.

"Mind if I tag along, then?" Cannon asked.

"Yes, I do. That's why we split up, remember?" Dram said.

"Well, I'll just follow along until we get to a clearing of some sort," Cannon said.

"And then, what?" Tam asked. Something about Cannon's story didn't sit well with her.

"What do you mean?" Cannon asked.

"What will you do when we get to a clearing?"

"I don't know. I'll think of something," Cannon said.

Dram picked up his plasma drill and slung the strap over his shoulder. He took the makeshift spear in the other hand. Tam picked up her spear and tools and walked beside Dram. Cannon followed behind them. She wouldn't say anything out loud, but his presence made her uncomfortable.

As they walked through the wooded area, the terrain

changed. She tried to gauge where the sun was through the canopy of trees, but it was difficult. She wanted to stay close to a water source since they had no way to carry water.

"Let's climb up this path to stay close to the river," she said.

"Good idea," Dram said. He handed her his spear and took the plasma drill and shot some holes into the rock surface. He let her climb up first, holding her spear and tools. When she got to the top, she reached down. "Hand me spears," she said.

She reached the tips and pulled them up. Then, Dram tossed her tools up and she caught them in her hands. She watched him climb part way up but he slipped back down.

"Hand me the drill," she said.

He slipped the drill off his shoulder and reached as far up as he could. She hung over the edge but couldn't grab the drill.

"I'll hold the drill for you," Cannon said.

"No!" she and Dram both shouted at the same time. Now she knew he didn't trust Cannon either.

"Turn it over and hand me the end with the strap," she said. She took the spear and reached down, snagging the strap. Carefully, she pulled the drill to her. The weight of the drill almost pulled her off the edge. Once it was close enough, she grabbed the drill and pulled it to her. She rolled over onto her back, clutching the drill.

"How in the world have you been carrying this drill?" she said. Dram reached down and helped her up off the ground.

He shrugged. She realized he was much stronger than he looked. Cannon appeared from behind. They continued walking along the river and the sky peeked through more open patches in the canopy. The river grew wider and an open patch of ground separated the river from the woods.

"Did you see where Tallie took us?" she asked Dram.

"What do you mean?"

"Did we go north or south?"

"I think we went east past the second set of mountain ranges," Dram said.

"Why does that matter?" Cannon asked.

"Because, when they brought me here, we came from the south. It was beautiful with lots of trees and villages and people," she said.

"We need to stay away from people," Dram said.

"Why?" Cannon asked.

"Because they will ask questions and want to know where we came from."

"They could also turn us in," Tam said.

"Right. I didn't think about that," Cannon said.

She got a good look at Cannon and realized he wasn't carrying his tools from the mines.

"Hey, didn't you have tools like me?" she asked Cannon.

"Yes, but I lost them when I saw the drone," Cannon said.

"What's that stain on your shirt?" Dram asked.

Cannon glanced down at the brown stain across the front of his shirt.

"I don't know. Maybe it's from the meat we ate with the dragon," Cannon said.

Dram glanced around, then grabbed Tam's arm and pulled her down to the ground. Cannon ducked down as well.

"What is it?" Tam whispered.

"I saw a herd of eeya up ahead. I want to get one for our evening meal," Dram said.

She watched as Dram crawled and inched his way toward the herd. He stood and took a shot with his spear. He hit one nearby and it went down. The herd scattered, running into the woods.

The three of them moved toward the dead eeya. Dram took out his rock tools and worked on skinning the eeya.

"Here, let me help you," Tam said.

Dram handed her one of the sharp stones and she helped him skin the eeya. She watched as he gutted the animal and cut off his head. She helped him carry the carcass on the skin toward the woods, leaving the guts behind.

While Dram rigged up a spit for cooking, she and Cannon found dead wood for the fire. Once Dram got the fire going, they rotated turning the meat. When it was her rotation, Dram went back to scraping the hide. He was relentless in his scraping.

"Can I ask you why you're doing this?" she asked.

"I'm making a blanket to sleep on."

"Well, that's a great idea," she said.

"Cannon, you better make some tools for survival before it gets dark because we're here, in a clearing. And this is where we split up."

"Oh, yeah. Maybe I can use some of the eeya bones when we finish eating," he said.

"Maybe," Dram said. He continued his scraping.

Tam watched Cannon sit, leaning against a large fallen tree, waiting to eat. There was such a difference between the two men. She tried thinking back on the night they ate with the dragons, but she couldn't remember the stain on his shirt. Dram did all the work. Yes, Dram's clothes were stained and grimy and smelly, but it was a smell she could live with.

She hadn't worked with Cannon in the past. He had been further away in the mines, but there was something about him that put her on edge. "You need to get off your ass and make a weapon for hunting eeya, because eeya bones won't be sufficient," she said.

He glared at her.

"You heard me," she said. She reached for her own weapon. "Something like this," she aimed it at him.

"All right, all right," he said. He got up and walked off. He appeared to be searching the dead wood around the area.

Dram glanced at her and smiled.

Later, when the meat was about done, the three of them ate their fill in silence.

Dram handed her a small piece of the hide. "This was the neck piece. Maybe you can make a pouch out of it."

She took the piece and studied it, then got some ideas. She broke off a small piece of eeya bone and sharpened it with her chisel and hammer, forming it into a sharp needle. Then, she searched the trees for thin roots growing around them. She chopped some of the roots off the trees with her chisel. When she returned to the fire, she began poking small holes around the edges of the piece of hide. She drew the makeshift string through every hole. Inside it, she put her chisel and needle. The hammer was too large. She poked a hole in the waistband fabric of her pants and pulled the root through it, to fasten the pouch to her pants.

"What do you think?" she asked Dram.

"Here, take care of these for me." He handed her the rocks he used to start a fire and those he used to skin out the eeya.

"You trust me with these?"

"Sure, why not," he said. He rolled out the hide on the ground. "You can share this with me if you want," he said.

"Thanks," she said. She sat on the far side of the fire.

"Move over." Dram pointed closer to the fire.

He trusted her more than she thought. She lay there, watching the fire and keeping an eye on Cannon, who lay across from her. Did he even find a piece of wood to make a spear? She sat up. "Where's my spear?" she asked. Dram handed her his spear and hers. He kept the drill between them. She lay back down and faced the fire so she could keep watch on Cannon.

Tam awoke at the sound of a strange noise. The fire was out. She sat up and saw Dram and Cannon fighting over the plasma drill. She grabbed her spear and pointed it at Cannon.

"Let go of the drill and you can leave in peace," she said.

Cannon glanced at her and laughed. Just as he did, Dram

hit him hard under the chin with the drill. Her spear raised over her shoulder, ready to throw, Dram grabbed her around the waist.

"Woah, we don't need to add to our crimes."

She glanced up at Dram. "You're right. I thought he was going to hurt you."

"Worried about me, huh?"

"Maybe," she said. She glanced around the area. It was still dark. Dram slung his drill over his shoulder and picked up his spear. She checked that her pouch was still attached and picked up her spear. She found a leftover piece of root-string and rolled the hide up, securing it with the root-string. She slung that over her shoulder.

Dram checked Cannon's pulse. "He's still alive."

They left Cannon where he fell and walked on through the night until they found an outcropping of rocks. Dram used his drill to carve out an alcove and the two of them bedded down for the remainder of the night. Dram drew Tam close to him. She liked his nearness and felt the warmth of his body. She fought off the mariposas growing in her belly. She wanted to enjoy being held by someone who cared for her and trusted her.

"I don't think Cannon was being truthful about the drone," Dram said.

"I got the same feeling. That stain wasn't there when we were with the dragons. It looked more like blood to me," Tam said.

"Yes, but whose blood?"

The next morning, Tam was up before Dram. She took care of her need to relieve herself. She saw Dram come toward her and saw something moving in the sky behind him. "What are those?" she asked. He turned to see what she pointed at.

"Those are scavenger birds. They circle like that when they've found something dead."

"That's not where we left Cannon, is it?" she asked.

"No, that's probably the eeya guts we left behind. Cannon was closer to the wooded area."

"I think I see something else in the distance," she said.

"Get inside the alcove," Dram said.

She crawled inside and Dram followed her. They pulled back against the wall and covered up with the eeya hide. "What do you think it is?" she asked.

"I hope it's not a ship searching for escapees, but Madda did say he destroyed a drone when we escaped the mine."

"So that was a second drone that Tallie burned?"

"Yes. So, they at least think someone escaped." Dram peered out from the side of their shelter. "It *is* a ship and they stopped near the scavenger birds."

Tam watched Dram's muscles flex in his arms and his back as he strained to lean out the shelter without being seen. He was in good shape for his age. If she had to guess, he was in his forties. He *did* say he had a son her age so he had to be twenty-eight anos. With his longer hair and dirty appearance, Dram looked much older.

"There are a couple guards searching the area," he said. He put his arm out to keep her back. "No, there's four of them and they're running toward the woods. They must have spotted Cannon." He sat back against the cold rock. "Be still."

They were quite a way from where they left Cannon. But Cannon would talk. Then they would know how many had escaped.

Dram peered out the side once more. "The ship is moving toward the woods. Damn!"

"What is it?" she whispered.

"They shot Cannon. The guards are dragging him back to the ship."

"We'll be looking over our shoulders for the rest of our lives," she whispered.

"Well, only until we find a way off this planet," Dram whispered.

"I like the way you think," she whispered.

Dram peered out once more. "They're heading back to the mountains."

Tam gathered their things and she and Dram headed for the woods, away from the river.

"They may return, once they realize how many bodies are missing," Dram said.

They continued walking for two more days, eating eeya and staying close to small streams until they came across some rocks that led to more mountains. These mountains were covered in trees and green bushes, where the others were only rocks. When they got near the top, they found a cave.

"Maybe I should start a fire so we can see what's inside," Dram whispered.

"Who goes there?" a deep male voice sounded from inside.

"Two travelers looking for rest. I'll share my eeya with you if you let us sleep in your cave," Dram said.

Suddenly, a bright fire rose up in the middle.

"Tallie? Is that you?" Tam asked.

"Have you seen Tallie?" the male voice asked.

"Not for a few days, but she helped us cross the mountain," Tam said.

"I'm Draco, Tallie's mate," he answered. A fire came to life within a pile of sticks.

"We could use your fire to cook our meat, but you can help yourself first," Dram said. He set the meat down in front of Draco, then slowly backed away. Draco took the meat in his claws and tore it in half. He handed half back to Dram. Dram set up some sticks to use as a spit. After Draco lit the pile of wood under the spit, Dram cooked the meat over the fire.

"Thank you, Draco," Dram said.

By now, they had two eeya skins to sleep on and another they used as a pillow when they weren't carrying their belongings. Tam had gotten better at skinning the eeya after she found some rocks she chiseled into sharp instruments.

By the time the meat was cooked, Draco had finished his portion of the eeya.

"Tallie said you were injured, but she didn't know if you made it," Tam said.

"Yes, one of my wings is damaged so I can't fly."

"Have you tried to reach her telepathically?" Tam asked.

"No, I haven't. I didn't know she was alive."

"Yes, and she lives in the mountains near the mines with Ruby," Tam said.

"Ruby?"

"One of her hatchlings. I kept her for a while until I met Tallie," Tam said.

"Why don't you try to reach her?" Dram said.

Tam sat up and called out to Ruby and Tallie telepathically. *'Ruby, Tallie, can you hear me? We've found your mate, Draco. He's alive and lives in the mountains where trees grow,'* she said.

Dram ran his hand across her back. "How did you get injured?" Dram asked Draco.

"Some evil people hunting dragons shot at me from their ship, but I took care of them. They won't be hurting anyone else again," Draco said.

"How did you take care of them?" Dram asked.

"I knocked their ship out of the air with my tail. They shot at me a second time and that's when they hit my wing. When they tried to escape their ship, I ate them."

"I'm sorry that happened to you," Tam said.

"Where is the ship now?" Dram asked.

"I hid it in the woods," Draco said.

"Do you mind showing it to us in the morning?" Dram asked.

"For another tasty eeya, I will. I have a hard time hunting without being seen these days," Draco said.

"You've got a deal," Dram said.

The next morning, Dram took Tam to hunt for eeya. When he found the herd, he pointed it out. He wanted to see if she could kill an eeya. She learned to skin an eeya, make new tools, and helped cook the meat. She did catch pesca their first day out, so he had confidence she could do this. She had to be able to survive if anything happened to him. After seeing the guards take out Cannon, their chances of surviving an encounter were slim. He watched her sneak up to the herd. She drew her spear up and heaved it into the chest of a big eeya.

"Good shot! Do you think you can carry it?"

She gave him a sideways glance. "We'll see," she said. She struggled to get under the thing to lift it up but she kept falling over.

"I'll help you with it since it's going to Draco. Here, you can carry the drill." He handed her the drill and watched her struggle to get the strap over her shoulder. She carried it across her body, instead of on one shoulder. Then she reached down and grabbed the back two legs.

"I said I'd carry it," Dram said.

"I know you did, but I'm helping you."

He picked up the front two legs and they walked up hill, back to the cave.

"That wasn't so bad, now, was it?" she asked.

"Work is always easier when it's shared."

He was impressed with her. And he thought about her more than he should. They set the eeya down in front of the dragon.

"Ah, just the way I like it," Draco said.

He watched as Draco downed the eeya whole. After belching a few times, Draco was ready to go.

The three of them walked along the ridge before climbing down on the other side. The descent was gradual. Draco stopped and removed some downed trees, exposing a shiny object. Dram moved closer and saw that the ramp was open. He carefully walked inside, his spear ready, along with his trusty drill. He searched for signs of life.

This was an older model. He searched the panels for information. There was no insignia on it, so it didn't belong to the I.S.P. or any officials.

"Nice Class C Cruiser, don't you think?" Tam said.

He turned to face her. "How do you know that?"

"It's on the ramp opening. Besides, I've worked on these," she said.

"Oh, have you now?"

Tam searched some compartments and pulled out a healing kit.

"What are you going to do with that?"

"Help a friend in need." She picked up a frequency wand and took it outside. Curious, he followed her.

chapter eight

"DRACO, LET ME SEE YOUR WING," Tam said.

He held up his torn wing.

"Dram, I'll need your help with this," she said. She showed him how to hold the two sides together. Then she waved the frequency wand slowly from the top of the torn wing to the bottom. It took some time, but a thin line formed, joining the two sides together. "Don't try to fly or use your wing just yet. We'll try this again tonight to strengthen the bond."

Dram went back inside and started the engines. Everything seemed to be working until he tried to pull the ship up. Alarms went off.

"Let me take a look," Tam said. She opened the hatch to the bottom and found the wires that caused the alarm. She followed them until she found a crack in the hull of the ship. She searched for tools to fix the crack, but there were none. Her chisel and hammer would do no good here.

"What are you looking for?" Dram asked.

"Something to seal up that crack," she said.

"Have you found any malloid rods?" Dram asked.

"I think so," she said. She went back to a cabinet she had opened before and found the rods. "You mean these?"

"Perfect," Dram said. He moved to the crack and slipped a rod in place. "Now all we need is a heat source," he said.

"Draco!" she said.

"Yes!" Dram was up the stairs and outside before Tam got there. He had Draco pull the ship away from the mountain side so he could inspect it for damage. It appeared to be only on the bottom of the ship.

"Tam, I'll need you to watch from inside and bang on the hull if you want us to stop," Dram said.

Tam headed back down the stairs. Once Draco and Dram got started, she could feel the heat through the hull. She watched the rod meld seamlessly into the ship. They started at the bottom, then moved up. She slipped a new rod into the crack as soon as the last one was finished. It took some time, but they finally finished. She headed back up when she heard Dram call out. "Help me cover this up, quick!"

She bolted for the ramp and found Dram and Draco covering the ship with large branches and a small tree. When she tossed the last branch on the ship, she saw something in the distance.

"Is that what I think it is?" she asked.

"Yes, this is the second time I've seen it. Get inside. Draco, you need to hide," Dram said. He shoved Tam inside the ship and closed the ramp.

"Help me work on the wires," Tam said. "We'll need to fix those before she'll fly." She climbed down the steps and Dram followed. Suddenly, it was dark. "What did you just do?" she asked.

"I covered the opening." A light flickered, then became stronger.

"What's that?" she asked.

"A light stick."

"Come here with that so I can see," she said. She searched for the wires and was able to locate the damage. Then, she rewired and spliced what she could. "That should take care of it," she said.

"All clear," Draco's voice sounded.

"I'm getting hungry," Dram said.

"Me, too." Tam followed him up the steps and down the ramp.

"It's getting late." She glanced up at the sky. "I didn't know it had taken that long."

"I'll get two eeyas tonight. One for Draco and one for us. We'll pack the leftovers for the trip," Dram said.

"Do you think the ship will make it out of the planet's atmosphere?" Tam asked.

"All the panels looked good. We'll check it tomorrow," Dram said.

The two of them hiked up over the hill to where the eeya herd had been earlier. They each got an eeya. That was the easy part. Dram hoisted his over his shoulders. Tam tried but couldn't lift her eeya. Dram set his down and helped her with hers so that she carried it across her shoulders. Walking with that extra weight was tough. How did Dram do that? If she had been on her own, she never would have made it. Then she realized they had to hike back over the hill to Draco's cave. "I'm not going to make it," she said. She called out telepathically to Draco. *Draco, we need your help with this eeya. It's too heavy to carry over the mountain.*

"You can do it," Dram said.

"Thanks for your confidence, but I reached out to Draco. I hope he heard me," she said.

Within minutes, Draco appeared at the top of the ridge. When he saw them, he raced to the bottom to meet them.

Dram gave Draco his eeya. While Draco dined on the meat, Tam helped Dram skin the other eeya. Dram rigged up a spit for cooking and Draco got the fire started. Dram took the first turn with the meat, while Tam ran the frequency wand across Draco's wing once more. She noticed the ridge that had formed earlier now blended more smoothly, making it hard to see the prior injury. "How does that feel, Draco?"

"Much better. Can I use it now?"

"Try moving it slowly," she said.

Draco moved his wing and then tried both wings. He lifted off the ground. He soared high above them and then returned to their camp.

"If you head west to the craggy mountains, you should be able to find Tallie and Ruby," Dram said.

Draco straightened. "I think I see them now."

"What?" Tam turned around. Something headed in their direction. *'Is that you, Tallie and Ruby?'* she asked telepathically. There was no response. "They aren't answering me! That may not be them," Tam said.

"Get down, Draco!" Dram shouted. He kicked out the fire and grabbed branches to cover the meat. Tam ran toward the woods with Dram behind her. She jumped behind a large bush and Dram joined her. He straddled her with his legs on either side of her and wrapped his arms around her. His closeness sent tingles throughout her body. Something she hadn't experienced before.

"Can you see anything?" she whispered.

"It looks like Draco. No, it's Tallie and Ruby. They landed in the clearing."

Tam heard a strange noise coming from Tallie. A deep guttural sound. She moved some branches to see Tallie walking around in a circle, making the noise. Then Draco flew in and joined her. He made a guttural sound as well, but it was deeper. They circled each other, while Ruby stayed a distance away, watching. Then Tallie turned her back on Draco and he jumped on her. She moved her tail and it looked like Draco was biting her neck.

"He's hurting her," she whispered.

"No, he's mating with her," Dram said. He spoke close to her ear and his breath sent another jolt throughout her body.

She felt his lips on her neck and the shock went down to her core. He kissed her neck and licked her.

"Do you feel that?" he whispered.

"Yes," she said, breathless. What was happening to her?

Dram moved away. "I'll be right back," he whispered.

Within minutes, Dram returned with a portion of the eeya.

"Let's go." Dram carried the eeya and she carried the spears as they headed to the ship. Careful not to loosen the covering, they walked up the ramp and then closed it. Dram set the eeya on a small table with two bench seats.

They ate their fill and Tam found some food compartments with cooling capabilities. She stored the rest of the eeya in the compartment and explored the ship. The feelings that Dram had awakened within her were running through her mind.

"I found a cleansing unit," Dram said.

"Oh, please let there be supplies," she mumbled.

"Ladies first," he said. He ushered her inside. She glanced around, tempted to be rid of this dirt and grime. "I have nothing clean to change into." She turned around and Dram was gone. She searched the larger compartments and found a sleeping unit.

"A bed, too!"

"And flight suits," Dram said. He tossed one to her.

She caught it and ran back to the cleansing compartment. She stripped off her ragged and dirty clothes and turned on the shower head. The unit had the sanitizing cleanser for hair and body. It took her a long while to scrub all the dirt off her body, but it felt good afterwards. This unit had a dryer to blow all the liquid off the body and hair. She pulled on the flight suit and fastened it with the magnetic strips that held it together.

She found another compartment with sanitizing mouth cleanser and used that. Then she gathered her dirty clothes and her eeya pouch with her tools and the frequency wand

and headed to the sleeping compartment where the two bunks were.

"Your turn," she said.

Dram moved very close. "You smell good," he said.

"I feel good, too. I'm going to fix this eeya pouch onto this flight suit, while you scrape all that dirt off you.

While he was gone, she took out the eeya bone she used for a needle and made a couple holes in the suit to accommodate her makeshift rope for her bag. She put her tools back into the pouch and realized she had been wearing the frequency wand in the pouch. Had the wand healed her of her past injuries when she was a child? She had never gone to a healer for the injuries her father inflicted on her. Could she be healed after such a long time?

Dram entered the room and she put those thoughts aside. She placed her pouch and tools in a compartment in the sleeping unit.

"Do you want top or bottom?" she asked.

"I want you," he said.

Dram moved toward her and pulled her into his arms. He kissed her neck and licked it as he had earlier. She tasted even better now, but she reacted the same. She liked his touch.

"It's been a long time for me, Tam, but I don't want to hurt you. If I do anything that hurts you, let me know."

She slowly nodded. He continued kissing her neck and moved toward her lips. He lingered there, exploring her mouth. Tam returned his kisses, tenderly at first, then more eagerly. He removed her flight suit and then dropped his on the floor. He led her to the bottom bunk, where he continued kissing and caressing her. Tam's flesh was smooth and soft, but her muscles were taut. While he caressed her, she did the same to him. She kissed his neck and chest and let him do the same to her. When he explored further, her breath caught and her hands dug into his back. "Am I hurting you?" he asked.

"No, this is all new to me," she said.

He kissed her tenderly and worked his way down her body, igniting a fire in her. When he entered her, her breath caught again and he slowly worked up his rhythm until she was ready for him. She moaned as he came inside her. Her arms reached around his back and squeezed him tight. He wrapped his arms around her, holding her tight for a few moments and then pulled her over on top of him. He caressed her back.

"How's that for an old man?" he asked.

She propped up on his chest. "Is that what love feels like?"

"Well, that's what it feels like for me," he said. He meant it. He hadn't let anyone get to him in all these years. The two of them cuddled for the rest of the night.

Tam was up early. She felt a little sore from the workout she had the night before and she smiled. She quickly cleansed herself and dressed back in the flight suit. When she had finished, Dram was up. He took his turn in the cleansing unit and she put her tool pouch back on. Today they would say goodbye to their dragon friends and then leave this planet. She hesitated at the ramp and decided to take her spear, just in case. Maybe she should wait for Dram. When she heard him leave the cleansing unit, she called out. "I'm heading to the dragon's cave to say goodbye."

"Wait for me," he said.

She stepped off the ramp and noticed the sky was overcast. It smelled like rain. Dram came up beside her. "Are you going hunting or visiting?" he asked.

"Visiting, but I thought I'd bring it just in case. Where's your spear? And your plasma drill?"

"Both are in a compartment inside." He covered the entrance to the ship with a large branch and walked beside Tam to the cave.

"Hello?" Tam called out. Tallie came out quickly, followed by Ruby.

"Where's Draco?" Dram asked.

"He went hunting this morning and hasn't returned," Tallie said.

"How long has he been gone?" Dram asked.

"Too long for my comfort," Tallie said.

"Too long," Ruby squeaked out.

Tam glanced at Dram. "Let's go look for him."

"Do you know where he is?" Tallie asked.

"Where you met him last night, is where we've been hunting eeya," Dram said.

Tam turned and headed down the path from the cave to the open field where the eeya had been grazing. Dram was beside her. Tallie hadn't seen them last night, so she didn't know they had watched their mating. Before she got to the bend in the path, she got a glimpse of something shiny. She drew back.

"What is it?" Dram whispered.

She leaned out and saw a ship in the field. "Damn, it's a ship."

Dram leaned over her. "Oh, no. They got Draco caught in a net. Do you have my cutting stones?"

"Yes. I've got our tools. Does Draco look all right?"

He held her as he leaned past the tree they hid behind. "He's pinned down and not moving. If he were dead, they wouldn't have a net on him."

"How are we going to rescue him?" she asked.

"If that's the warden, we aren't."

"What do you mean? Draco's helped us. We can't just leave him."

Dram turned around and leaned on the tree. We've got to

come up with a plan. We can't just barge in there. We don't know who that is."

"Well, if it's the warden, what would he want with a dragon? And if it's dragon hunters, we can take them out."

Dram glanced back at the scene from behind the tree. "There's one guard outside that I can see and he's watching Draco."

"Does he have a weapon?"

"Yes, it looks like a laser rifle. We can't defend against that."

"How good is your arm?" Tam asked.

"What do you mean?"

"How far can you throw a rock?" She tossed a good-size rock up in the air. Dram grabbed it.

"We'll have to get closer if you want me to knock him out," he said. The two of them slipped into the wooded area and moved closer to the ship.

"We can't get any closer or he'll see us," Dram said. He pulled his arm back and threw as hard as he could. The rock hit the man in the head, knocking him out. Dram moved toward the man to grab the rifle, while Tam moved toward the net. She cut through the netting where the pegs were. Dram pulled up the pegs on his side.

A movement from the ship caught her attention and she motioned to Dram. He spun around and shot the man coming down the ramp. Draco moved under the netting and pulled up the rest of the pegs. Another man came running down the ramp and Dram shot him as well. He checked the first man he knocked out with the rock. His flight suit had no insignia on it and the ship had no markings. Dram went to check on the two men he shot. Tam retrieved their laser rifles.

"There are no insignias. They could just be dragon hunters. Draco stayed at the entrance while the two of them moved up the ramp. No one else here.

"Maybe we should hide this ship like Draco did the other," Tam said.

"I'm thinking they may have tracked that ship. There could be others in the future."

"Draco, you aren't hurt, are you?"

"No. They caught me off guard. And I think you are right, Dram. Is there any way to remove the tracker?" Draco asked.

"There might be. I've got to get into the engines and see what's there," Dram said.

"I can help you with that," Tam said.

The two of them climbed down to the engine room and searched for some type of tracking device. After tracing each wire from start to finish, Tam found something unusual on one of them. This ship had some tools on it and she was able to remove the device.

"Now we need to check the other ship for a tracker," Tam said. They closed everything and when they left the ship, Draco was at the bottom with Tallie and Ruby.

"We wanted to say thank you and goodbye," Tam said.

"Thank you for helping Draco and bringing us back together," Tallie said.

"You're welcome. I will miss you, Ruby," she said. Ruby came up to her and tried to lick her. "You've grown so much!"

"Thank you both for your help. We will never forget you," Draco said.

"It's you we need to thank, Draco. You found us a way off this planet. You take care of yourselves and be careful. One more thing," Dram said.

"What is it?" Draco asked.

"Help us push this ship into the woods," Dram said.

Tam held a laser rifle on each shoulder and put more tools into her pouch. She watched Dram, Tallie and Draco push the ship as far back into the woods as possible.

"I will cover it up when you leave," Draco said.

"What happened to the men that were here?" Tam asked.

Draco belched. "Well, I couldn't let a good meal go to waste, now, could I?"

"You didn't!" Tam said.

"We did," Tallie said. "We were hungry and they were dead, so, no waste."

Dram and Tam headed back up the hill to where the other ship was. "We'll have to remove that tracker as well," Dram said.

Tam tapped her pouch. "We've got tools this time."

chapter nine

TAM FOLLOWED the wires on the repaired ship and found a similar device. With the new tools, she was able to remove it herself. While she was down in the engine compartment, she searched all the wires to make sure there were no other devices or problems with the wires. She had experience in tampering with these wires on other ships, so she knew what to look for. When she was through, she climbed back up to the top and set the lid in place.

Dram was at the Nav-U-Com, going over the systems in pre-flight. He had already closed the ramp and put up the new weapons and her spear. She sat beside him.

"I take it you've flown before?" Dram asked.

"Yes, but they didn't trust me alone," she said.

"Why is that?"

"I sabotaged the ship trying to kill Berto."

"While you were on the ship?"

"Yes."

"That took guts. Now that Berto is not part of the equation, you'll help me, won't you?" Dram asked. He started the engines.

"Of course I will. I trusted you with my body last night, why wouldn't I help you now?" she asked.

"Good point. Neither of us can fly this ship alone for long. We've got to eat and sleep some time."

"Got it."

Once they were 100 kiks in the air, something in the distance caught their attention. "That looks like smoke," Tam said.

Dram glanced at her. "We can keep going straight up and leave this planet," he said. He touched her shoulder.

"Or we can see what's happened and maybe help someone?"

"You know where that is, don't you?"

"The prison?" she asked.

"Yes. If we go back, they will capture us and that's the end of our story," Dram said.

"Maybe, it's a new beginning for both of us," she said.

Dram took her hand and pulled it to his lips and kissed it. "Last night was our beginning."

She smiled. "Don't you believe in redemption?"

He squeezed her hand and let go. He moved the throttle forward and they headed back to the prison.

The warden's guards dragged Cannon in front of the group of survivors in the area where they had their mid-day meals.

"What we have here is an escaped prisoner. I want you to see what we will do to escaped prisoners," the warden said.

He grabbed Cannon by the hair and yanked his head back. Then he whacked Cannon across the chest with a whip handle. Cannon grimaced in pain. Both arms were held by two different guards. The warden continued hitting Cannon across the chest, his legs, and then arms with the whip handle.

"You can let him go, boys," the warden said.

The guards stepped back while the warden used his whip

to tear into Cannon's flesh. After several minutes of lashes, he stopped.

"You can tie him up over there, boys," the warden said. He pointed to a rock wall across from the entrance to the prison.

Cannon was spread-eagle against the rock with his hands and feet anchored to the wall with restraints. His clothes were bloodied from his ordeal.

"Now, if anyone else gets the idea they want to escape, this is what will happen to you."

One of the regular guards left the area. The warden motioned for another guard to come forward.

"What is the status of the search for prisoners?" the warden asked.

"We've recovered thirty men alive on levels one, two and three. But we lost ten men so far," the guard answered.

"You **lost** ten men? How did you **lose** ten men?"

"They were crushed by the rocks, sir."

"No one missing from those levels?"

"No sir. We recovered the bodies of the deceased, so everyone is accounted for."

Kellen came running out with the guard that had left.

"What's the meaning of this?" Kellen pointed to Cannon.

"He's an example of what I will do to escaped prisoners. He's to have no food or water the rest of the day, do you understand?" the warden said.

"I understand perfectly." Kellen glared at the warden.

"Guards! We will continue our search. Let's go." The warden turned and left with his four guards.

Kellen waited until they had left on the warden's ship. "Help me with this man," Kellen said. Two guards joined him in removing his restraints. "Let's get him to the med bed," Kellen said. They carried him inside and got him to the healer. They put Cannon into the med bed.

"It's going to take a while to heal these injuries. Who did this?" the healer asked.

"The warden. Let me know when his condition changes," Kellen said. He headed back to his office and notified the committee.

A few minutes later, a thunderous boom and shaking began. The shaking continued for several minutes.

"Jardan, status report!" Kellen shouted into the comm-link.

"The large drilling equipment was crushed beyond use in the quake, sir. We'll have to get another drill to get to level four," Jardan said.

"Did the drone show any survivors?" Kellen asked.

"No, sir. We were hoping to retrieve the bodies."

"What about level five and six?"

"Nothing on level six from the last drone report a couple days ago. Level five may have survivors. I will check that now."

Jardan punched in the level five drone commands and sent the drone searching for survivors. There was no movement, but there were heat signatures. He counted ten. "We have ten survivors with possible injuries on level five, sir," Jardan said.

"I've called in for another drill. I hope it gets here today, otherwise, we may lose everyone on level five," Kellen said.

"Have you checked all the levels of the prison, sir?" Jardan asked.

"Yes, everyone is out in the patio," Kellen said. Kellen thought about the possibility of another quake and the loss of men in the mines. He contacted the prison farm on the southern part of the planet. He alerted them to his problem and what the warden was up to.

"I'll send you a ship to bring the men here. We can accommodate them," Tiller said.

"Thank you!" Kellen said. Then he contacted Jardan.

"Jardan, I'm moving these prisoners to the prison farm in the south for safety. Come to my office."

When Jardan arrived, Kellen was pacing the floor.

"Yes, sir?"

"Jardan, I want you to find some prisoners who will volunteer to help you search levels four, five and six. Enough to help retrieve bodies or help the injured. I'm leaving the healer and one med bed for any injured prisoners. The new drill and three operators should be here any moment," Kellen said.

"Will you be back, sir?" Jardan asked.

"Yes, and I'll pick up survivors and the med bed. We can no longer operate safely in these mines. Once I get the others settled in, I'll be back. I'm taking the three guards that are left, so it's up to you."

"Yes, sir."

After Jardan left the office, Kellen went to check on Cannon.

"He looks much better," Kellen said.

"Yes. He's been confessing while he was unconscious," the healer said.

"Confessing?" Kellen asked.

"Yes, sir. There were five others that escaped," the healer said.

"Did he mention any names?"

"He seemed to be reliving some experiences. Someone named Madda was eaten by a dragon."

"What?"

"Yes sir. Apparently, there's a dragon on this planet. And two others, Keo and Kragg, fought him about something. The way he moved around on the bed, he might have killed them."

"How much longer does he need to remain?" Kellen asked.

"I think he will be fine, sir, but I would shackle him for your safety," the healer said.

"I agree. I'll send in another guard to take him. I want you to stay for the others who will need healing. We've got another drill and operators coming in to search the last three levels," Kellen said.

"Yes, sir."

By the time the ship arrived, so did the big equipment. Jardan supervised the lowering of the drill into a new section of the mine, but it had to drill past the first three levels to get to level four. It was time-consuming and the oxygen level in the level five mine was dwindling since the cave-in.

Between the equipment and the drone on level four, Jardan was able to guide the operators in the search. He directed four of his volunteers to search with the help of a Hover-Trol and illuminators. They retrieved three bodies, but no survivors.

"We can't get to the people mover. It's been crushed badly," one volunteer responded.

"Can you tell if there's anyone in it?" Jardan asked.

"No sir, it's so flat you can't get a comm-pad in between the rocks."

The drill had a small people mover on it and brought up the three bodies, first, then the four volunteers.

Jardan looked over the bodies. He was missing Bronin, one of the guards; the female prisoner, Tam, Cannon, who was in a med bed, and Kragg. For Tam's sake, he hoped the warden didn't find her. He added that information to his comm-pad to send to Kellen when he finished his search.

Once the bodies were taken care of, the drill continued working down to level five. It was another hour before they reached that area and Jardan had to guide them with the drone so as not to injure anyone further. He picked up some movement in the level when they heard the drilling. "Take it slow, boys, we don't know had badly these men are injured," Jardan said.

It was slow going for another hour before they could lower the people mover. He sent two men down to assess the injuries.

He watched with the drone as they checked the prisoners. They sent three at a time who were ambulatory back up in the people mover. He directed the other volunteers to help get the injured to the med bed. They would have to take turns since there was only one here. He could see that the remaining prisoners were struggling, so he sent two more volunteers down to help get them to the people mover.

They came up two at a time. Jardan took the comm-pad with him and went to help remove the injured to a Hover-Trol and then up to the med bed area.

"I'm going to need help here," the healer said.

"Once I get everyone out from level five, I'll be back to help you," Jardan said. He couldn't spare any of his volunteers, at least, not yet.

After another hour or so, he had all the live prisoners out and at the healer's room. There were three dead prisoners, so he had each volunteer bring one up until everyone was out of level five. The last volunteer brought up the drone.

"One more level," Jardan said to the drill operators. They began work on the final level by continuing down from level five. He ordered all the volunteers to assist the healer until he needed them again.

While they drilled, he re-worked the drone to use on level six. Then he headed to the healer's room to check on things there.

"Everything is fine here, but it will take a while to get to everyone," the healer said.

"How many men do you need to finish your work here?" Jardan asked.

"I can get by with two of them," he said.

"The four of you, come with me," Jardan said to the remainder of volunteers.

They headed to the outside of the mountain where the drill was. He gave the drone to one of the operators to send down in the people mover.

Using his comm-pad, he checked the progress of the drone as it went down into the shaft. He could see the bodies of at least three people. "I'll go down with you," he said to the volunteers. He wanted to see the tunnel that had been made and see if anyone was still in it.

Once he and two others got into the level six mine, they located all three bodies. The people mover inside the mine was crushed. They loaded two bodies into the drill's people mover, along with one volunteer. While they waited for the return of the people mover, the mine shook. Jardan sent the drone through the tunnel that had been made to see where it went.

Finally, the people mover returned and he and the three volunteers loaded the last dead body into the mover. The mine shook more violently and the people mover closed before he could get inside. He watched it pull up and he turned to climb through the tunnel. He had his comm-pad with him and could see the drone had reached daylight. He continued crawling through until he reached the outer edge. When he climbed to the top, he could see the drill pull up out of the shaft while the mountain shook again.

The volunteers pulled the bodies from the people mover and took the Hover-Trol with the bodies down to the bottom of the mountain.

Before Jardan could wave to the operators, the mountain shook again. He watched in horror as the drill slid down the mountain. The operators jumped away and the drill crashed down in front of the entrance to the prison and exploded into flames.

Jardan joined the three operators on the top. Without the

Hover-Trol, they couldn't get down the mountain without climbing down the hard way.

Off in the distance, Tam could see something coming toward them. Another ship? Her heart skipped a beat. "I hope that's not who I think it is," she said.

Dram glanced at her. "Are you thinking it's from the warden?"

"Yes!"

"They don't know who we are, remember?"

"I hope you're right," she said.

Moments later, a voice came over their comms unit.

"This is Plumaris Prison Patrol and you are flying in Prison airspace, identify yourself," the voice said.

"It sounds like the warden!" Tam said.

"This is Dragon Patrol One, come in," Dram said.

Tam bit her lip to keep from laughing.

"Dragon Patrol? There is no such thing," the warden answered.

"Believe what you want, we're checking the safety of our dragons. Do not attempt to harass or stop the dragons from their everyday activities."

"Who is this?" the warden asked.

"Dragon Patrol out."

Dram pulled up and flew above the warden's ship.

Tam glanced at the monitor. "They are now following us," she said.

"Time to leave the atmosphere," Dram said. He pulled up and left the atmosphere of the planet. They stayed just above the atmosphere and waited.

"Do you think they'll follow us?" Tam asked.

"I hope not."

They waited half an hour and headed back to the prison.

The warden's ship was nowhere in sight.

Dram landed the ship a distance away from the main entrance, which was engulfed in flames. The dark smoke rose up above where the doors used to be.

"I can't see anything beyond the flames," Tam said.

She saw a movement out of the corner of her eye and turned toward it. "Look! There are people on that ridge," she said. "It's the ridge we came out of when we escaped."

"Let's go!" He grabbed her hand and they ran back to the ship. Within seconds, they were at the ridge, hovering above the heads of the four people.

"Can you land here?" she asked.

"No. It's not level. You'll have to help them into the ship," he said.

Tam ran for the compartments, searching for something to pull them in. All she had was her spear. "This will have to do." She punched the panel next to the ramp and it lowered. She walked out onto the ramp and lowered her spear. "Grab the end and I'll help you up," she shouted.

The man was heavy with something hanging from his shoulder. She barely pulled him to the ramp before falling on her butt. The man was able to pull himself onto the ramp.

"Jardan?"

"How did you get this ship?" he asked.

"I'll explain later. Help me with these men," Tam said.

"I have an idea." Jardan walked past her and tied his rope onto the frame of the ramp and lowered the rope.

"Good idea," she said.

One at a time, Jardan and Tam pulled someone onto the ramp.

"Go inside and sit down," Tam ordered.

Finally, after all the men were on board, Jardan leaned over the ramp. "I think we got everyone." He walked inside with Tam and she closed the ramp.

"Where to?" she asked.

"Take us to the patio on the other side of the mountain," Jardan said.

Tam headed into the Nav-room and let Dram know where to go.

"Are you sure?" he said.

"Yes. Jardan is with them." She helped Dram as they travelled the short distance back to the patio area. When they arrived, she and Dram went to let them out.

"Dram?" Jardan said.

"Uh, hello Jardan. What's happened at the prison?"

"Let's get these men off the ship, then we'll talk."

Tam went down first and the men followed. "Wait here for Jardan," she said. She walked back up the ramp.

"We lost a fourth of the prisoners due to the first quake. When we finally reached the sixth level, we had several other quakes. There was no one alive on the sixth level and the opening we made with the big equipment caved in. I went out the tunnel you dug."

"Those plasma drills came in handy," Dram said.

"Yeah, I found two of them at the exit. These men escaped the big drill before it slid off the mountain. It exploded and caused the fire," Jardan said.

"Did you send a drone out looking for us?" Tam asked.

"We sent two. The first one was destroyed in the mine," Jardan said.

"Yeah, Madda took that one out and told me about it later," Dram said.

"The second one got as far as the mountain when it was hit by fire. Do you know what happened to that one?" Jardan asked.

"Tallie took that one out," Tam said.

"Tallie?"

"A dragon friend. She took us across the mountain and we split up," Dram said.

"A dragon?"

"Yes. You wouldn't know anything about dragon hunters, would you?" Dram asked.

"No. I didn't know there were dragons on this planet."

"Well, it's a small family and they are our friends, so don't do anything to hurt them," Tam said.

chapter ten

A SHIP CAME in from the south. "Uh, Dram?" Tam said.

"I see it. It's time we left. You understand, Jardan, don't you?" he asked.

Jardan grabbed Dram's arm.

Tam grabbed Jardan's other arm. "Please don't let the warden take me," she pleaded.

"That's not the warden. It's Kellen coming in from the southern Farm Prison."

"What?" Dram asked.

"He came back for the rest of us," Jardan said.

"Couldn't you tell him you found our bodies in the mines?" Dram asked.

"No, we pulled all the bodies out. Everyone's accounted for except you two, Madda, Keo and Kragg," Jardan said.

"Madda was eaten by a dragon," Dram said.

"And Cannon knows what happened to Keo and Kragg," Tam said.

They watched Kellen's ship land and then another ship came up from behind them.

"No!" Tam shouted. She ran toward Dram.

"You can't let him take her," Dram said. He wrapped his free arm around her.

Jardan watched Kellen's ship before glancing at the warden's ship.

"Let us go, please," Tam whispered. Jardan studied her face.

The three drill operators stood glancing between both ships when the healer and more prisoners came out to join them.

Her ship was between Kellen's and the warden's ship. Maybe she could make a run for it, but she wouldn't leave Dram behind. And Dram hadn't made an effort to escape. She noticed that Jardan had no weapon.

The warden got out first. "How dare you escape this prison!" the warden said. "Take them!" he ordered his two guards.

"Jardan, please!" Tam shouted.

Jardan turned toward the warden. "These two didn't escape. They rescued me and the three drill operators. Don't touch them."

One guard glanced over his shoulder at the warden.

"You have orders!" the warden shouted.

The guard pointed his weapon at Jardan. Tam ran behind Jardan, but the other guard grabbed her.

Dram reached behind Jardan and punched the guard in the face. The other guard whacked Dram with his rifle butt, knocking him out.

Tam jumped across Dram's body to protect him. "Don't touch him!" she shouted.

Jardan shoved the guard who had grabbed Tam and managed to get his laser rifle. He turned just in time to see the warden with his whip and another guard coming toward him.

The two guards grabbed Tam, pulling her off Dram and dragging her toward the warden. They stopped in front of the warden. Each guard had her by the arm. The warden ran the handle of his whip down her chest and stopped at her core.

"Tie her up," he said.

Jardan turned and waved the healer and a couple of prisoners over. "Get him to the med bed through the side entrance," he said. The three of them did as they were told.

Jardan aimed the rifle at one of the guards tying up Tam's arm to the restraints that had held Cannon earlier. He felt a hand on his shoulder and turned to see Kellen beside him. Kellen had four guards with him, all holding rifles, ready to shoot.

"Warden, you are relived of your duties by the authority of the Council of Nations," Kellen said. "You will release Tam now or suffer the consequences."

The warden turned toward Kellen. "You have no authority over me, Kellen—"

Just as the warden spoke those words, Draco swooped down and swallowed him whole.

"Yes! Thank you, Draco!" Tam shouted.

Tallie flew in behind Draco and blew fire at the guard who had tied Tam up to the restraints, catching his clothes on fire. Then Ruby did the same to the second guard. Her flame had gotten bigger and so had Ruby.

Jardan and Kellen glanced at each other. "Get her down from there," Kellen ordered two of his guards. "Jardan, go arrest the warden's rogue guards. Put them in restraints and bring them to the ship."

"Yes, sir!" Jardan said.

When Kellen's guards brought Tam to him, she said, "Don't hurt my dragon friends. They helped me and Dram. If you are kind to them, they will be kind to you, too."

"Are you all right?" Kellen asked her.

She nodded. She would be much better if she knew Dram was all right. He took a hard blow to the head. And if she hadn't talked him into coming back and helping, they would both be off this planet. Now she felt bad for suggesting it.

"Come with me," Kellen said. He took her by the arm and

led her inside the prison, through the side entrance. He turned to one of his guards. "Help these men load up on the ship." The guard left and took all but the healer and another prisoner with him.

Kellen guided her to the med bed area. Dram sat up, speaking to the healer. She ran to Dram and he put his arms around her. They clung to each other for several long minutes. It was as if no one else was there but the two of them.

"Are you okay?" Tam whispered.

"I am now." Dram stood up from the med bed. The healer and the one prisoner moved the med bed out of the healing room.

"I'll help them load the med bed into the ship," Jardan said.

Tam realized it was only her and Dram and Kellen left in the room.

"Wait here until we are in the air," Kellen said.

"And then what?" Dram asked.

Kellen pulled the door open and glanced back over his shoulder. "Live a good life and stay out of trouble." Then he was gone.

Tam's mouth dropped open. Dram grabbed her and spun her around. Then he lifted her up and kissed her.

When Kellen's ship was fading in the distance, the two of them walked to their ship, holding hands.

Sitting in the Nav-U-Comm, Dram turned to Tam. "Where to?"

"Let's try a galaxy I've never been to," she said.

"Hmm. I know just the place." Dram set the controls for the Pleiades. He pulled up on the throttle and together, they headed for the stars.

dragons of lun

Chapter One

This was Danner's last mission searching for the slaves, together with his team. Afterwards, they would all go back to law enforcement throughout the galaxy. Berto, Shey, and Coz had been great teammates. The four of them had found all the slaves that Dram had sold and returned them to their home planets after the slaves had been healed from their trauma.

But this last mission was different. The information gleaned from Dram's records didn't show a sale of humans. It just had an entry—Lun.

Lun was a moon of Tarsius, same as Ti. Berto and Coz were both Tarsians, but neither of them had been to Lun. Danner had been to Ti with Adam and Genesis and that moon was teaming with dinosaurs. What was on Lun?

From his own research, all he could find out was that Lun was habitable. A small group of people from Tarsius had flown to Lun over ten anos ago, but no one had heard from them since then.

"Danner, are you still awake?" Berto asked.

"Yes, I couldn't sleep."

"Well, you've got the Nav Room in a couple hours. Do you want me to fix you some capu?" Berto asked.

"Sure. I might as well," he said.

Berto went to the small galley and fixed three cups of capu. "Do you want to join me and Shey in the Nav Room?" he asked. Berto handed him a cup.

"Sure. We can talk about the mission," he said.

***

After settling down in the Nav Room, Danner sipped his capu. "What are your thoughts on this mission, Berto?" he asked.

"I don't know why Dram had put Lun on his records. That was before I was blackmailed into working for him. He either wanted to go there or he did something there," Berto said.

Shey glanced at Danner. "I looked over your research. Did you want to go to Tarsius first and check out the village of Lugat to see if anyone remembers anything?"

"It's been ten anos," Danner said.

"There should still be people there who remember something," Berto said.

"Sure. That's a good place to start. Set a course for Lugat," Danner said. He finished his capu and stood up. "I think I'll nap a little before my shift. See you in an hour or so."

Danner headed to his bunk. He had a sleeping unit to himself. Before Tam was arrested, Berto and Coz shared a unit and Shey and Tam shared a unit. Now, it was Berto and Shey, since they were mates and Coz had his own unit. They had to make modifications to Berto's unit and put in a larger bed to accommodate two people. That was unusual, but both of them were good I.S.P. agents and it was worth it in the long run.

Within minutes of his head hitting the pillow, he was asleep. When his alarm went off an hour later, he bolted out of bed. He rubbed his eyes and tried to shake the fog that shrouded his brain. *Where was he? What was he supposed to be doing? Ah, yes, the mission to Lun.*

He freshened up and headed back to the galley. He made two cups of capu and headed to the Nav Room.

"Is that for me?" Coz asked.

"Yes, it is." He handed one of the cups to Coz and they stepped inside the Nav Room.

"How's our progress?" Danner asked.

"Twenty-one hours to Lugat," Shey replied.

"Sounds good. We'll take a day off in Lugat to re-supply the ship, then we'll head out to Lun," Danner said.

***

Twenty-one hours later, Danner set the ship down just outside the village of Lugat. The four of them walked to the village and found some shops that were open.

"Hola, que quiere?" the shop keeper said.

Berto replied in the Tarsian dialect. "Queremos comida para nuestra viaje."

Danner handed Berto the list and some credits. He walked around the shop as the two spoke. This shop only carried food. He watched as Shey went out to another shop. Before he could see what Shey was up to, Berto handed him and Coz some bags of food. Once they left the small shop, Shey came up to them.

"I found someone who might be able to help us," she said.

Danner and the others followed her to the another shop.

"He speaks Vaedran dialect," she said.

"Can you help us?" Danner asked him. He was an older man, sitting on a stool outside the shop.

"Yes," he said.

"Do you know anything about a group of people that left this village over ten anos ago?"

"Yes, I do. They left for Lun. They wanted to explore and make a new life for themselves. They weren't happy living in Lugat," the man said.

Shey glanced around. "Lugat seems like a fine place to live," she said.

"I thought so, too, but they didn't like the authority here and wanted to be their own bosses."

"Have they been in touch with you since they left?" Danner asked.

"We haven't heard anything from them since they left."

"Do you remember who left? Was it males or females or both?" Danner asked.

"It was both. My son and his mate, along with several of his friends and their mates."

"How many of them left altogether?" Berto asked.

"There were about twenty altogether," the old man said.

"We're going to Lun to find them," Danner said.

"If you do, tell them they are always welcome here, even if they just want to visit," the old man said.

***

The four of them headed back to the ship to put the food up. Danner couldn't shake the feeling he had that something was about to happen. Something was about to change, but he couldn't figure out what it was.

After the food was put away, he thought that maybe he just needed a little diversion. He remembered the Galactic Bar and Grill was on the space station above Tarsius. This would be the closest they would be to the station. Since Berto's sister owned the Bar and Grill and Coz had a thing for her, he didn't think anyone would complain if they went there. "We're heading to the Galactic Bar and Grill for a good meal and a good night's sleep. Tomorrow, we head for Lun," he said.

***

After landing on the space station, Mariposa greeted them at the entrance to her establishment.

She hugged Berto and Shey, then turned to him and gave him a hug as well. "How are you, Danner?"

"I'm good, and you?" he asked her.

"Perfect now that you are all here," she said.

Coz wrapped his arms around her and they hugged more warmly than all the other people she hugged. They exchanged a passionate kiss. Watching them was a little uncomfortable, reminding him of his own loneliness. It was a matter of time before the two would become mates. *Had Coz even asked her to be his mate?* He would have to check with him on that later.

Danner shook off his loneliness. He had seen a lot of his I.S.P. teammates become mates for life and wondered why he hadn't been as lucky.

Mariposa escorted them to a table with a great view of space.

"I'll get your mesero," Mariposa said. She left them to themselves.

"So, this mission is to determine whether or not Dram had anything to do with the people on Lun, is that correct?" Shey asked.

"Correct," Danner said.

"So, if he *did* have something to do with it, what then?" Coz asked.

"If part of the group is missing, we'll have to track them down and bring them back after their healings," Danner said.

"Like we did with the others?" Berto asked.

"Yes."

"So, after this mission to Lun, will we be finished with the missions?" Shey asked.

"You're going to Lun?" the mesero asked.

"Yes, why?" Danner asked. He noticed the worried look on the mesero's face.

"You don't want to go there, trust me," the mesero said.

about the author

Ester López has been writing for over 30 years. She lives in
the Smoky Mountains with her husband, their dog, Chewie,
two mini horses, Pepper and Bucky, and some crazy chickens.
When Ester isn't writing, she's either photographing flowers
and landscapes, sewing, doing stained glass, making crafts,
working in her flower gardens, canning, or making wine.
To keep up to date on Ester's book releases, and to get the
FREE "Vaedra Chronicles Companion Book," please join
Ester's READERS GROUP and follow her Blog at:
www.esterlopez.com
Follow Ester on:
www.facebook.com/EsterLopezAuthor or on X at:
www.x.com/esterlopez1 or Instagram at:
www.instagram.com/esterlopez2956
And if you like the story, please leave an honest review at
your favorite bookseller.
You can also join Ester's Group Page on Facebook at
Virtual Book Signing & Takeover Group

also by ester lópez